SLIVERED

Slivered Souls Trilogy

KANDI VALE

Dea,
It was <u>soo</u> wonderful meeting you! Happy reading ♥

xoxo
Kandi Vale

Slivered (Slivered Souls Trilogy)
Copyright © 2018 Kandi Vale, all rights reserved.
This is a work of fiction. Any resemblance to actual persons, living or dead, is entirely coincidental.

Please purchase only authorized editions of this book, and do not participate in or encourage electronic piracy of copyrightable materials.

Cover by Jenifer Knox
Interior design by Raven Dark

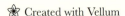 Created with Vellum

CONTENTS

Acknowledgments	v
Prologue	1
Chapter 1	5
Chapter 2	11
Chapter 3	18
Chapter 4	26
Chapter 5	28
Chapter 6	34
Chapter 7	40
Chapter 8	50
Chapter 9	57
Chapter 10	63
Chapter 11	69
Chapter 12	75
Chapter 13	90
Chapter 14	94
Chapter 15	99
Chapter 16	113
Chapter 17	124
Chapter 18	130
Chapter 19	135
Chapter 20	141
Chapter 21	148
Chapter 22	151
Chapter 23	155
Chapter 24	164
Chapter 25	170
About the Author	181

Acknowledgements

To my husband, who pushed me to chase my dreams and supported me every step of the way. I love you more. Always.

To my very first fan, Lisa. Without your encouraging words and hilarious GIF's, I wouldn't have pushed so hard to make this a reality.

To my first beta reader, Jenny, thank you for being the ultimate cheerleader.

To my muses, Britt and Heather. Thank you for the late night brainstorming sessions, love, and support.

To my mentor, my graphic goddess, and dear friend Jenifer, thank you for everything you have done for me and Slivered. Words are not enough.

To my editor, Tanya Oemig, your skills take my breath away. I can't wait to continue working with you on Kisa and Dolor's story.

Formatting done by the amazing Raven Dark.

This list could go on and on. I have had so much love and encouragement from my friends and fellow authors that it completely melts my heart thinking of it. None of this would have been possible without all of you. Thank you.

Now, let's go dance in our darkness.

Thus the heavens and the earth were completed in all their vast array. (Genesis 2:1)

Prologue

In the beginning, God created angels. They were resplendent, magnificent creatures, save for their pride. Even so, God was pleased. That pride, however, began to fester, and with it came something God had not anticipated. His angels, these beings of perfection, could feel pain. Rage swept across the heavens and conflicts arose. The skies became infested with an emotional and physical darkness. These shadows wrapped themselves around the very heart of God's kingdom and began to squeeze the glory from it. Amidst the bickering and struggles, God soon realized the need to eradicate this darkness. He created a being of light. A beast whose sole purpose was to devour the pain of others, taking their darkness into himself and healing them in the process.

All was well, for a time.

This beast created by God did his duty brilliantly, absorbing the immense pain the angels gave him and yet received no acknowledgement for this kindness. He came when they called and was dismissed just as quickly. Kept chained in the Narliu caves, the beast felt the pain taking residence in his soul. Just as it had with the angels, the pain and rage built, dampening his light. The energy he gained from his feedings consumed him, as did his loneliness.

A watchful gaze noticed his growing strength and despair and decided the beast would make a mighty pawn. The manipulations of one lonely being would change the course of destiny forever.

The Beast's paws made no noise as he prowled through the legion of angels. His ebony fur shimmered off their gold plated armor, his reflection a constant reminder that he didn't belong. He paused at the front of the line for a moment before stepping forward, moving several feet away from the mass of soldiers. Lucifer separated from them as well, stepping up beside him. Together, they stared out over the open stretch of heaven.

They were vastly outnumbered. God's army swelled before them, thousands of wings blotting out the sky as they surged towards their own small fraction of rebels.

Lucifer looked down, reaching forward and snapping the golden collar from the Beast's throat, as had been promised. She slid the golden harness into her armor and gestured out towards the incoming herd of bloodthirsty angels.

"Now you shall keep your end of our bargain." Her words were cool, challenging him to disobey.

The Beast had no intention of breaking his word, however, and walked further out towards the masses.

With a mighty roar, the Beast lashed out at the charging army with all the pain he had gathered over the past few months. Lucifer had taught him how to harness the pain; to let it swell within him. It exploded now, and the Beast could do nothing but watch as the creatures he had served his entire life fell before him. They clawed at their armor as they writhed, wings broken from the fall to the grassy terrain. Screams the likes of which the Beast had never known ran across his fur, and he felt his shoulders curve. He lay down on his front paws, a whimper coming out of his massive throat. He had healed these beings for millennia. What was he doing? Maybe this weakness he felt now was his punishment for such an atrocious crime. He had only wanted his freedom...

"Good. Now take it back." Lucifer looked down at him. Her words were laced with excitement, and the Beast knew he had laid a fatal blow to the opposing legion. "Do it. Now!" Lucifer snapped.

They had discussed this before the battle, but now the Beast felt so weak...

Lucifer grabbed him by the scruff of his neck, jerking him around to meet her eyes. The blue flames in them made the Beast recoil. "You are no longer a prisoner. You are free. Now fight for that freedom. Those sniveling cowards do not deserve your strength. Take it back!" She released him, her eyes boring into the Beast's.

The Beast saw many things in Lucifer's eyes. Sadness, rage, defiance, and madness swirled in their crystal depths. There was also the memory of Lucifer first calling upon him. Telling the Beast that she could offer him his freedom. Telling him that he deserved more than an eternity of servitude to a bunch of ungrateful sycophants. Lucifer had then done something no one else had ever done. She offered the Beast a name. All of these things flickered in that gaze, and Lucifer seemed to be able to track those thoughts.

She leaned forward again, placing her hand on top of the Beast's broad head. "Dolor Comedenti. Take back your fate, my friend."

The soft words seemed to snap something deep within the Beast's chest. He rose, looking out over the still screaming angels. As Lucifer had advised, the Beast focused on the pain he had unleashed, and as he had been beckoned for centuries, he called it back to him. It whirled around him, so much more than he had sent out, and still he called. He felt the energy fill him, felt the angels' screams turn to simple whimpers.

"Don't stop. Take it all." Lucifer whispered, and the Beast listened. He didn't know how these things worked, but he trusted Lucifer. He drank in that dark energy until he thought he might erupt with it. Lucifer began to laugh.

With a shuddering gasp, the Beast felt the last bit of pain seep into him. He collapsed onto all fours, his breaths ragged. He looked down at his paws, eyes widening as he realized they were paws no longer. Lifting those strange appendages, the Beast could only stare at the long fingers clenching and unclenching before him. He glanced down his torso, shocked at the long, lean, hairless body. His new hands trailed down his skin, and he felt a shocked bark of a laugh leave him. He looked up at Lucifer who smiled down at him.

"Rise, my friend. You kneel before no one." She offered him a hand, and the Beast rose shakily onto unsure feet.

Exhilaration pounded through him as he straightened, his skin nearly glowing with power. He raised his eyes at the eerie silence surrounding them. As his gaze raked over the army of corpses scattered across the ground, Dolor took a step back.

He had gained a name and lost his soul.

Chapter One

"They are coming for you, child. Evil has awoken, and they will not stop. They are coming."

Kisa blinked down at Mrs. Mary Kosinski, the elderly, if not ancient, resident currently occupying room 102 in the memory care unit at St. Francis Memorial Hospital. The woman's ivory hair was made up of brittle pale wisps, messily curled upon her head. It had probably been quite some time since she had been to the salon. Kisa looked down at Mrs. Kosinski's frail but determined fingers gripping her wrist, noticing that her salmon colored nail polish was chipped nearly clean off. Making a note to remind the volunteers that were in charge of prettying up the residents, Kisa smiled gently, attempting to remove those withering fingers, and wincing as the woman's nails dug slightly into Kisa's pale flesh.

"Mary, I'm here for your x-ray. We are just going to take a quick picture of your chest, okay? The doctor wants to check out that cough." Her voice was calm and reassuring as she finally managed to loosen Mary's fervent grip.

Mary's eyes were a stunning crystal blue and surprisingly clear today. She had been a favorite of Kisa's ever since she had entered the hospital with a badly shattered femur. She had tripped over "those damn pixies" as she had put it, and declared that she was fine and just needed to sleep it off. Kisa still got surprised at the strength in these old birds. Hell, she had men big as legends come in, howling in agony over injuries, their cries of "it's broken, I know it's broken" echoing off the lead doors. Thank goodness Kisa mastered the blank face years ago, or she would have a hard time when the x-rays developed, showing perfectly intact bones. Then there were patients like Mary, who just wanted a shot of bourbon and some rest.

"Bah, it's just a damn cough." The woman waved her hand dismissively. "I don't need no stinking x-ray. Do you know how many of those things I've had?"

Kisa nodded, knowing exactly how many, since she had been doing most of them. Kisa worked the day shift, and desperately tried to get the memory unit x-rays done so that second shift didn't have to deal with the sundowning when these residents were the most combative and difficult to deal with. Mary, while not limited on feistiness, had never gotten physical with Kisa before, until today.

"I know, Mary, but the doctors are worried about you getting pneumonia again. If that happens, you're going to be stuck here with us even longer. I know how much you want to get home." Kisa smiled softly, twisting the laptop of her machine around to face her. She pulled up Mary's information. Kisa set up her equipment slowly, plugging in her portable unit so it could warm up. She wouldn't do the x-ray if Mary resisted, but if she got the go ahead, she wanted to move as quickly as possible. Kisa had learned from experience that the longer these conversations went, the more upset the patients got. "What do you say, Mary? Can I shoot a quick picture so we can get you feeling better?"

Mary's brows furrowed, clearly disgruntled. "Oh, fine. If you must." This is how their conversations always went, and Kisa knew what would come next. "My grandson used to do this, you know. Brilliant boy. So smart. You would like him. Maybe you can meet him when he comes and visits me. He should be here any day, you know."

She felt the familiar pang of sadness at Mary's words. She never received visitors, and it made Kisa's heart clench. Kisa internally rolled her eyes at the fairly obvious attempt at playing Cupid. She was used to the residents trying to play matchmaker, but it never seemed to get less cringeworthy. If Kisa had been looking for a man, which she certainly wasn't, it definitely wouldn't be someone who never visited his ailing grandmother.

As she rambled on, Kisa checked the computer, seeing it was ready for exposure. Kisa nodded and moved the bedside table off to the side, then leaned Mary forward in her bed to place the cassette behind her back. "Oh, that's cold. And it hurts my back. Hurry up!" Kisa quickly placed her machine, instructing Mary to lift her chin. She watched Mary's breathing, the rasping breaths lifting her stomach subtly. She knew better than to tell Mary to take a deep breath. If she did, Mary would just breathe more rapidly, and then it would be practically impossible to get a decent shot.

After the exposure was taken, Kisa pulled the cassette out and got her equipment together, tucking it away and sliding Mary's rickety table back to her side. She bit back a curse as one of the wheels stuck, tipping the table slightly. Kisa grabbed at a falling glass of water, catching it right before it could soak the book lying beside it. The novel was dog-eared about halfway through and Kisa couldn't resist glancing at the title, smirking as she noticed the half naked man on the front.

She lifted a dark, delicately arched brow at Mary, who scoffed. "I'm old, not dead." Mary picked up her reading glasses, propping them on her bony, age spotted nose. Kisa shook her head, leaving Mary to her smut books. The old woman probably thought about sex more than she did, which admittedly wasn't much.

"Skunk oil."

She paused at the door, glancing back at Mary in

confusion. She looked at Kisa over her glasses. "For the klutziness, child. A touch here." She pointed to her left shoulder. Kisa glanced at the rows of elaborate oils lined up on a small table in the corner of Mary's room. She would rather be a klutz, she thought.

"And Frankincense for those evil hordes. Let the girls know I would like some tea, please." With that, Mary dismissed her, turning back to her romance novel.

On her way out, Kisa let the nurse at the desk know about Mary's nails and the tea. She headed to radiology and tried to push back the strange interaction with Mary. She seemed to be getting worse, and it weighed heavily on Kisa's mind. She had never known her own grandparents, and her attachment to the residents both eased that ache and created new ones.

Back in the solitude of the radiology department, Kisa sighed as she finished her enormous amount of paperwork. She knew that if she just scanned it in throughout the day, it wouldn't be nearly as overwhelming. Procrastinator through and through, however, she just never could make herself do it.

It was finally Friday, and the weekend couldn't have come soon enough. The week had left her feeling exhausted, and she just wanted to go home and curl up with a good book. Kisa vaguely wondered if all the reading she had done would end up leaving her like Mary, old and gray, fantasizing about pixies and evil.

Closing her eyes for a moment Kisa let her mask slip, the exhaustion seeping from her bones as her shoulders drooped. She was drained, her sleepless nights catching up to her quickly. The nightmares were getting worse. Some days it took her hours to realize that she couldn't escape them. She was living them. This horror story of pain and numbness had become her life, with no exit sign in sight.

Maybe she should try therapy again. She reached down and instinctually snapped the rubber band on her wrist. The painful snap was supposed to bring her back to the present, according to the shrink she had gone to a whopping two times to appease her parents. What good did that do when the present was what tortured her so?

Kisa jumped as Hanna, her coworker and friend, flopped down onto the dingy chair beside her, the wheels creaking.

"How was she today?" she asked. Hanna knew Kisa had a soft spot in her heart for the old broad.

"Relatively clear-headed. She didn't ask for Charles once, which was a relief. Oh, I am going to be attacked by evil hordes of unknown origin though." Kisa smirked, tucking her papers into the bin to be recycled later.

Hanna snorted, spinning slightly in her chair, her bleached blonde hair looking pale in the harsh office lights. "Last week she told Mallory that she has a chopped up ogre buried behind her refrigerator." Kisa shook her head, her dark ponytail swaying as she glanced up at the emergency room screen that hung above their desk. Sighing in relief, she noticed it was practically empty.

"I'll take fantasy delusions over the other ones any day of the week." Their faces were somber as they recalled some of the other residents, the ones who did nothing but beg for help that would never come. Kisa couldn't imagine having to work in those units, day in and day out. Going down there every few days was trying enough, physically and emotionally.

She scolded herself as she thought of the poor souls trapped inside of their own heads. Things could always be worse. What right did she have for such self-pity? It had become her mantra lately. Things could always be worse. Right.

Hanna stood abruptly. "Come on, I'll treat you to lunch. If you are going to be scooped away soon by evil boogeymen, it's the least I can do."

Kisa smiled, walking over to the silver lockers to grab her purse. "How could I say no to that?" Oh, she wished she could. Her mask had to be snapped into place and touted out regularly, lest her secret despair be revealed. Her soul screamed as she chatted with her friend about hospital gossip, her pain raking furious claws down her ribcage at being denied its due acknowledgement.

Chapter Two

"This is a terrible idea," Mattheus grumped for the hundredth time. Dolor rolled his eyes at his friend, ignoring his petulant rant. They trekked through the cold woods, the two pale blue moons casting eerie shadows in their wake.

"Seriously. Why did we think this was a good idea?" They broke through the clearing, panting and staring out over the coast before them. The sand was nearly white in the daylight, but under those cerulean orbs it seemed to glow the light blue of Earth's skies. They continued across the beach, heading towards the black water crashing against the shore.

"We need access to this realm, Mattheus. Stop bitching." Dolor dropped the heavy chest he was carrying at his feet, the blue poof of sand enchanting in the moonlight. Mattheus grunted as he dropped his own chest, the loud thump drowned out by the angry tide.

"Well, we could have negotiated more." His accent, which was as close to Brazilian as Dolor could pin down, thickened in his agitation. He tugged his coffee colored fedora down tighter on his head.

Dolor took in his longtime friend and business partner. At six feet two, you would think the muscled brute would have nothing in this world to fear. His cocoa colored skin looked pale in the dim shadow of the moons, and Dolor watched him swallow nervously.

Dolor sighed, his long frame dropping down onto the sand. "Mattheus, sit." He needed to get his friend calm before the negotiations began. Dolor was not a charmer. He preferred to take what he wanted and ask questions later. He was the fear behind the operation, the brute force that pushed the realms to cooperate with what they were trying to build. The legend of him was enough to make most happily agree to terms. Mattheus was the charm, the smooth talking businessman that could run circles around contracts. They needed each other to make things work.

Mattheus plopped down beside him, his fingers burrowing into the sand. Dolor watched with a sad smile. He knew this trip would be difficult for his partner, but he hadn't fully anticipated how much. The Vepo realm was Mattheus' home. A home he hadn't seen for centuries. He had fled his position, refusing to be tied down to a legacy he didn't want.

He rarely talked about the home he had left behind, but watching him gaze up at the enormous moons, Dolor knew his pain ran deep. "Do you regret it?" he asked him, his voice quiet.

Mattheus closed his eyes, breathing in the salty breeze. "Yes and no. I could never have been what they wanted me to be." He looked at Dolor then, his emerald eyes sober, but determined. "I don't regret it. How could I, with what we've built?"

Dolor smiled at him, nodding. They had created something that no one else could have. They had made a market, farming and producing goods found in the Other Realms. No one else could travel to the Others. No one but Dolor, and he had capitalized on this fact. There were only three realms left, and they would have access to them all. The empire they were forging was immense, and the power they were accumulating was a heady thing.

"Then let's get this over with. Drinks on me tonight if

we land this contract." Dolor stood, brushing the sand from his midnight suit. It was as expensive as Mattheus', although they held little affection for such material things. The suits, the contracts, the charming faces they presented… they were all pieces of a chess game. One they were quickly dancing across with ease.

Mattheus snorted. "We own the club, asshole. Drinks are always on us." He stood and followed him as the first pale head breached the water.

Dolor watched as Mattheus pushed his shoulders back, his mask snapping into place with a bright smile. He waved at the approaching creatures walking to the shore from the shallow water.

The three beings were a wash of white. From their platinum hair, to their pale skin, to their willowy clothing. The only color came from their overly large brown eyes and the garish gems that wrapped about their necks. A crown with purple black stones rested on the short woman approaching in the middle.

She was stunning, her gown clinging to the curves of her luscious body. Her iridescent skin seemed to glow in the moonlight just like the sand. Perhaps it did. Dolor would have to ask Mattheus later. She paused in front of them, and Dolor and Mattheus bowed. Mattheus flung an arm out dramatically, his eyes twinkling up at the Princess of the Selkies, his previously betrothed.

"Princess. Thank you for meeting with us on this beautiful evening." Mattheus reached forward, grabbing her hand and kissing the back of it softly, his eyes never leaving hers. Dolor nearly snorted. The princess gave away nothing, her muddy eyes cold as she stared down at him. A man and woman stood on either side of her, watching the display with furrowed brows.

"Rise, Prince Mattheus of the Encantados. I hear you care to make a bargain?" Her voice had a watery lilt, and Dolor could practically feel the slide of seaweed across his flesh. He held back a shudder, but barely.

They both straightened, towering over the three selkies in front of them. The selkies were a type of shifter. Their other form was that of a massive seal with razor-sharp teeth. Dolor was proud of Mattheus for hiding his flinch at her address. He tried very hard to forget that title. Seems they hadn't here.

"That we do, Princess. We wish to open trade with your people." He smiled down at her, his eyes telling her that's not all he wished to do. Her cheeks pinkened barely, and Dolor scented her desire and rage on the breeze.

"Do you now?" she purred, her eyes sliding down his body. "Tell me, Prince, why would I wish to trade with someone with no honor?" Her words were as brittle as the rocks the sea crashed on, cutting Mattheus deeply, though he wouldn't show it.

Instead, Mattheus tossed his head back and laughed. "Oh, Princess. Can we not let the past be the past? You and I both know we had no say on the betrothment. It was not my honor I sullied, for I made no oath to you. It would have harmed your honor, however, if I had followed through with a courtship I did not have heart in." His words oozed sincerity, and Dolor saw the princess shift, some of the tension leaving her. Dolor had often wondered if Mattheus held some sort of compulsion magic.

"We have made this same contract with hundreds of Other Realms. They have all been satisfied with our services thus far." Dolor's voice was low and firm. While Mattheus charmed and wooed the client, he would reel them in with his confidence and will alone.

Her eerie eyes focused on Dolor, taking his measure the same as she had Mattheus. "I know of you, Beast. You think I should trust you? I hear you are but a savage."

Dolor grinned, letting the savage show in the baring of his teeth. Fuck, he hated that name. Every time someone called him Beast he wished to rip the tongue from them. He couldn't afford the rash anger now though, so he shoved it back, only letting it flicker in the depths of his eyes.

"Oh, I am certainly that, but that doesn't change a binding contract." He felt the two with her stiffen, magic gathering to them in their fear. The fear slid down Dolor's throat like a fine wine, and he felt the predator in him revel in it. The princess did not look afraid, however. She stared at Dolor and nodded slowly.

"Very well. If you had lied and tried to come across as something but yourself, I would have cut this meeting quite short. I do not have time for games. What are the terms?"

He chuckled softly. If only she knew the games they were playing. Mattheus wisely spoke up before Dolor could respond. "Terms are fairly simple, my lady. You will have access to trade with any of the Other Realms that are contracted to us. We will take a percentage of those trades for our profits and act as the middle men for your transactions." Medicines, magics, plants and herbs, creatures… All was up for trade. With the goods they commandeered, they then had bargaining chips for all realms. The Others hadn't seemed to put together that they were unintentionally giving the two of them access to monopolize the market.

"What percentage?"

"Twenty percent. With a guarantee of delivery." Dolor's teeth gleamed with his response.

"Seems a bit steep," she muttered, looking towards her silent companions.

"As a token of good faith…" Mattheus stooped down and unlatched the forgotten trunks at their feet, flinging back the lids.

The selkies gasped and inched forward, curious gazes captured by what lay inside the chests.

"From the Earth realm, my lady. I believe the humans call them Swedish Fish." Both chests were filled to nearly overflowing with an assortment of the colored, jellied candy. Shaped like little fish, they shimmered and beckoned to the fish loving shifters.

The princess looked up with a bright smile, her teeth suddenly looking much pointier behind her full lips. "Eighteen percent and you have yourselves a deal, gentleman."

"Done." Dolor nodded, pulling the contract from his jacket pocket.

The princess read through the contract and then had each of her lackeys do so as well. Dolor shoved his black hair back off his face, the dampness in the air making it stick to his forehead. Finally, she nipped her pale thumb and placed the wound against the bottom of the page. Deep brown blood soaked in, instantly morphing into a delicate signature. Mattheus did the same, and the bargain was sealed.

"If you ever change your mind, Prince." The princess raked her gaze down Mattheus' long frame once more before turning and heading back into the murky depths, her hips swaying against the turf.

"Fucking Casanova." Dolor plopped an arm down on Mattheus' shoulders, relieved that the deal was done. He had had serious concerns when setting up the meet and greet. He thought the Princess would demand a ring on her finger. By the relief shining on Mattheus' handsome face, he knew he had not been the only one thinking it.

"You owe me a drink," Mattheus groaned as they turned, heading back towards the woods. Neither of them noticed the jade eyes that watched them from the water.

Chapter Three

Kisa shut her studio apartment door firmly behind her, leaning against the cool metal. She slid down, her head resting back as she sat, bringing her knees to her chest. The room felt cold, and she realized she had left the air conditioner running. She stared across the sparse apartment, eyes dull as she noted the mess. Dirty scrubs and sweatpants lay scattered throughout and her roller derby bag sat in the corner, the stench of the unwashed pads seeping through the heavy material. She was going to wash them after practice last week, and the week before that. She closed her eyes, shutting out the mess and the emptiness. She allowed her mask to fall, that fake sense of normalcy slipping from her features. Her eyes opened, and the hollowness she felt was all-consuming. She numbly surveyed her apartment, her eyes landing on the picture atop her chestnut coffee stand.

Adam's head was tossed back, his military cut, blonde hair gleaming in the sun, his straight white teeth dazzling in the stretch of his smile. Kisa sat beside him in the tall grass, gazing up at him with clear adoration, smirking at his reaction to the joke she had just told him. He always found her hilarious, even though her jokes were terrible and her sense of humor particularly quirky. His tanned, muscular arms rested around her shoulders, and she leaned into him, as she usually did. They were normally touching whenever they were together. A slight trace of fingertips, a brush of shoulder…

What was the joke that she had told him? She dug through the emptiness of her thoughts, reaching back to that day. They were having a picnic, her father across from them. He was the one who took the photo. Her heart, which she didn't think could break further, chipped again as she realized she couldn't remember the words that caused that raucous laughter.

Her phone beeped, and she blinked, dazed. She reflexively swiped at her cheeks, though her tears no longer fell. She didn't miss them, which said more about her current state than anything else. She reached into the front pocket of her scrubs. Noting the new text message, she startled slightly at the time. It was 5:15 p.m. She had been sitting there for over an hour. Opening the text message, Kisa read her father's barely legible text. That poor man would never get the hang of it.

Hi r yuo still piking me up at meeting

Kisa stood, feeling the ache in her legs as she headed to her room. She had to get out of this apartment, and out of these scrubs. She shot back a message, letting him know she would be there to pick him up at seven. Grabbing a black t-shirt from the floor, she pulled it to her nose, smelling it and looking it over. Smelled okay. No food, anyway. Kicking off her tennis shoes and socks, she changed into the t-shirt and a wrinkled pair of jeans. Her attire was in a sad state, and she remembered a time when she had actually enjoyed shopping. Enjoyed the feel of putting together the perfect outfit. Now her wardrobe consisted of plain t-shirts, jeans, sweats, and scrubs.

Heading towards the door, she picked up her keys from the floor and searched for her flip-flops. Finding them in the kitchen for some odd reason, she slipped them on and left. She didn't give the photo a second glance.

Kisa pulled into the parking lot of Abner's Adventures at a quarter to six. It was the only bookstore she had ever known to be open 24/7. Abner, the owner of the store, lived below the quaint shop. Kisa turned off her car, leaning her head back against the worn seat and closing her tired eyes. She needed a few minutes to collect herself. Abner always had a way of seeing right through her if she were too frazzled. As she focused on putting her mask firmly back in place, Kisa remembered the first time she had discovered the shop.

It was small, the bookshelves reaching to the low ceiling, with barely enough space to walk between them. When she had first entered, the claustrophobia that had swelled within her threatened to make her turn right around and walk out. She had begun to do just that when a kind voice reached her through the books. She squinted, ducking her head to look between two shelves to her left. Sure enough, two of the brightest blue eyes she had ever seen stared back. The wrinkles that surrounded them only seemed to enhance the color, as a gentle voice spoke between the shelves.

"A bit daunting, I know. I have tried to put a leash on 'em, but they have a mind of their own." Those enchanting eyes peered upward, trailing across the thousands of books lining the small space.

She could hear the shuffling of feet as those eyes disappeared, and a man came around the corner. He was hunched with age, nearly bald with small tufts of white hair escaping beneath the temples of his round glasses. He smiled at her with kind eyes as he reached out, his fingers bent with arthritis.

"My name is Abner, but you can call me Abe. I run this mess of a store."

She returned his small smile with one of her own, taking his hand. His grip was gentle, and yet firm. "I'm Kisa. It's nice to meet you, Abe." He tilted his head, stepping back and leaning on a small wooden cane she hadn't noticed before.

"Kisa, eh? That's Russian, yes?"

Kisa nodded, watching as a knowing smirk lit his face. "Yes, my grandfather was from Russia. My mother was always fascinated with the culture, even though she had never been there." Kisa shook her head slightly. Her mother's eccentricities never ceased to amuse her.

"Ah, a wanderer at heart! My kind of lady! So, Kisa, what can I do for you on this fine day?"

Kisa nodded at the books, eyeing the intimidating stacks. "I'm looking for a new book, but the selection here is a bit... overwhelming."

Abe chuckled, following her gaze. "Nonsense! You just have to know where to look! Now, fiction or non?"

"Fiction, please. Fantasy, if you have it?" She didn't need any more reality in her life. Her own reality was plenty.

Abe looked at her as if she had just said something particularly amusing.

"I think I may have a book or two of that selection." He turned abruptly, heading down the aisle and turning sharply left. She followed, staying close so as not to get lost in the behemoth maze of novels.

After several more twists and turns, Abe stopped, pushing his glasses up the bridge of his round nose as he leaned in close to a section of books. His crystal eyes squinted as he read the title. "Ah! Here we are." He slid the book from the crowded shelf, and Kisa felt her heart stutter as the shelf groaned loudly, the books all shifting as dust fled the nooks holding them in place. Abe didn't seem to notice her discomfort as he beamed up at her, holding out the dusty cover. Kisa took the extended book, turning it sideways to read the title on the spine. *The Adventures of Kelpies*. She smiled, looking up at him.

"Kelpies huh? Don't think I've ever read this one…"

Abe's smile broadened, his wrinkles growing more pronounced. "Wonderful! Now, you take that and bring it back when you're finished." He nodded and turned away, heading back through the books towards the center of the store.

"Wait! I haven't paid you yet!"

His voice sounded distant as he called back through the store, his voice muffled by the ancient books. "Hogwash. Didn't you know, my dear? This is a library as well. Be sure to bring it back, will you? That's my only copy." And then he was gone.

She did bring it back a week later, and had been visiting the strange bookstore, or rather library, every week since. Taking a deep breath, Kisa grabbed her latest book from the front seat, locking her car and heading towards the welcoming building. She had plenty of time to exchange books and pick up her dad at seven.

"Abe?" Kisa called out as she entered, the tinkle of the copper bell above the door barely audible. A small meow was the only response, and Kisa looked down to see Abe's calico cat, Sherlock, weaving between her feet. She picked him up, petting him gently. "Where's the boss man, Sherlock?" she muttered to him, making her way down the aisle. Sherlock merely purred, snuggling closer. She normally did not like cats, preferring dogs, but she would make an exception for this ball of fluff.

Kisa heard a scuffle towards the right and headed that way. Even though she had been visiting the store for months, she still felt like the bookshelves were never in the same place, and worried often about getting lost. Silly to feel that way in such a tiny store, but feel that way she did.

"Abe?" she called out once more, rounding another corner. She heard a startled yip and the thud of books.

"Oh, my word! Goodness gracious, Watson!" Abe clearly sounded frazzled as Kisa rounded the corner, noting the books scattered across a rickety table and the floor. They looked newer than the others, and she smiled at the old man's hoarding tendencies. The last thing he needed was more books.

"I hope you plan on selling these." Kisa smiled, leaning gently against the nearest bookshelf, watching Abe as he straightened.

He returned her grin, his white button-down shirt untucked and covered in dust. Slipping off his glasses, Abe cleaned them on his filthy shirt and perched them back on his nose. They were still smoky with grime.

Kisa shook her head, walking forward and putting down the disgruntled cat. She slipped the glasses off his nose gently, cleaned them on her relatively clean t-shirt, and handed them back to the flustered man.

"Oh, yes, my dear. These were a special order. Watson decided to go exploring through the stack, it would seem." Frustrated affection lined his words, and Kisa leaned down, glancing under the table at the chubby black tabby curled on top of a blue hardcover. Shaking her head at the feline, Kisa straightened, grabbing the small paperback from under her arm.

"Oh, yes! How did you like this one? Those pesky pixies can be quite entertaining, eh?" Abe's voice was alight, the way it always was when he spoke of his precious adventures.

"It was fun, although I wish Sally would have been a bit stronger at the end. No way should she have ended up with that meathead, Thomas." Kisa wrinkled her nose, hating the weak damsel in distress cliché.

Abe looked aghast, his thin mouth dropping open in horror. "It's a romance, Kisa. You can't have a romance without a happy ending." He shook his head in disbelief, taking the book from her and heading for the correct shelf.

She followed him, staying silent. She hated romances, and she wished her throat didn't feel tight at the prospect of asking him not to recommend them anymore.

His steps slowed abruptly, and she nearly collided with his back, lost in her own thoughts. His eyes swept up the tall shelf, settling at the top row. "Be a dear and grab me the ladder, would you?"

Kisa walked further down the row, grabbing the old, small ladder and bringing it to him.

She watched nervously as he climbed it, instinctively stepping behind him. His face was serious as he eyed the collection before him, carefully grabbing a dark leather novel from the shelf. As he came back down, she noted the lack of sparkle in his eye that usually resided there. He gave her a small smile and handed her the book. She glanced down, her brows wrinkling. It felt... cold in her hands. She looked up, searching for the vent.

"You might want to check into having these books moved, Abe. If there is a vent nearby, the moisture will damage them." Abe nodded, looking tired.

"Will do, hun. Now, you run along. I'm going to get these books ready for pickup and take a nap I think."

"You feeling okay?" Kisa asked, concerned.

Abe scoffed. "Of course, dear. I'm just old." He smiled, some of that twinkle returning.

"Okay, well be careful on that ladder. I'll see you next week."

Abe nodded, turning and heading back to his scattered

collection. Kisa left, worry settling deep within her. She was fond of Abe and she knew firsthand how quickly old age could creep up on someone. Thoughts of Mrs. Kosinski and her failing health did not brighten her mood any. Consumed by these thoughts, she completely forgot about the book resting coolly against her torso.

Chapter Four

Kisa absently fiddled with the radio station as she sat in her car outside the meeting hall. Plants accented the outside and wooden picnic tables lined the front. People milled about, smoking and talking among themselves. The NA meeting was over, and she waited for her dad to come out, knowing he had probably gotten caught up with one of the other members. He liked to play the mentor role to the newly sober, and while Kisa found it endearing, it also made her worry endlessly. Her father had one of the softest hearts she knew and got attached rather easily. It wouldn't take much to tip him back to his own demons.

Her eyes found the book lying in the seat beside her. She picked it up, frowning at the chill that still lingered there. The cover was nearly black, with a strange symbol on the front. She looked at the spine but found no title. She jumped slightly as the passenger door opened and her dad's tall form folded into the front seat.

He was in his fifties, slim, but with the muscle and deep tan of long years and hard labor. The baseball cap that was always present hid his slightly receding hairline that he desperately tried to ignore. He carried a narrow Tupperware container, the red lid covering his tobacco and rolling tubes. A cigarette rested between his lips, and he rolled down the window when he settled into the car, knowing that Kisa hated the smell of cigarette smoke. He leaned over, kissing her on the cheek. She smiled warmly at him. "Hey, Dad."

"Hey, pumpkin. Thanks for the lift."

"Where we headin'?" Kisa asked, starting the car.

"Can you head over to Mike's? I did some work for him on that rental and he owes me some cash. I could kind of use it."

Kisa nodded, pulling out. She listened to her dad's directions, enjoying the low rumble of his voice. He had one of those voices that would have been great for relaxation audio tapes, the rough cadence soothing somehow.

"Kisa? Did you hear me?" That voice was now laden with concern, and Kisa forced her wandering mind to focus. She hated to cause him any worry.

"Sorry, dad. Long shift at work. What were you saying?"

His concerned frown didn't lessen, and she knew he could see right through her. He always could. "You know, pumpkin, you could go to a meeting with me sometime. It might do you some good. Get some shit off your chest. I know things haven't been easy since…"

"Dad. I'm fine. Really. I'm just tired today." She cut him off, having no desire to hear this lecture again.

"Yeah. Sure. Okay, then." Her dad turned and looked out the window, his shoulders hunched. She hated it when he pouted, and hated herself more for causing him to pout. Why couldn't he just act like everything was fine like she did? She sighed and reached over, grabbing his hand. He looked back at her, and she felt her heart clench at the tears in his eyes.

"I miss him too, pumpkin." His words trembled with the emotion there, and Kisa felt like the worst daughter in the world. She knew her dad felt pain at the loss much like she did. What was worse was that she couldn't be there to comfort him. She couldn't even comfort herself. Instead, she merely held his hand tighter, knowing that it wasn't enough. That it would never be enough.

Chapter Five

Kisa stared up at the rough, wooden ceiling. The floor was cool against her overheated skin. Suddenly, a light green face was looking down at her, a large smile showing brown, even teeth. Kisa blinked, then blinked again. How hard was she hit? The face was now just a normal, pretty one. White teeth, not brown, inside a pale, square face. Slam pushed her glasses back up the bridge of her nose, reaching down and offering a hand. "You alright, K? It's not like you to be picking daisies."

Kisa took the offered hand, shaking her head as she got up. "Picking daisies" is what they called it when a derby girl wasn't paying attention to what was going on around her. It was a favorite of Kisa's, to knock down someone who didn't have their head in the game. She had been off all day, missing jammer after jammer. If she didn't snap out of it, she was going to be benched the next bout.

Kisa had been seeing things. Weird things. She wondered if maybe she had gotten a head injury in the last bout. If she didn't have such terrible white coat syndrome, she would have gone to the doctors to be checked over. Instead, she just kept trying to ignore the strange things that had been popping up. What's that small, humanesque thing flying around her head while jogging? It must be a new species of dragonfly. A one-foot tall, blue guy at the grocery store? There must be a smurf convention in town. Kisa was a pro at avoidance. Now it was messing with derby, however, which was unacceptable.

"Maybe you just need to get laid," Smack suggested as

they geared down, done with practice for the night. Kisa tensed, hiding it behind a smirk.

"I think you're projecting, Smack." She chuckled, hurriedly shoving her equipment into her bag, She did not want to have this discussion.

"True." Smack sighed. "But nonetheless you need to get some too. We need you on top of your game for this next bout. We need to beat them by at least fifty points to secure our ranking. That means you need to get over this funk, girl. Go out with us tonight. We're checking out that sexy spot over on the water." The girls consistently tried to lure Kisa into their adventures and sexcapades. They meant well, and Kisa had almost told them about Adam just to get them to stop. She never did though. She couldn't stand the thought of the girls looking at her with pity or thinking she was weak. Here, on the floor, she was strong. Fierce. She could take on any skater and come out on top. She wanted her real life and endless despair to stay far away from here. Maybe that's what made her speak up tonight.

"What club?" Kisa inquired. Everyone paused. The silence made Kisa squirm as she tucked in her helmet. Was she really such a recluse? Yes, yes she was.

Smack recovered with ease, trying not to let her eagerness show. "It's called Restless. It has the hottest waiters, hottest club goers, and kickass music." Kisa snorted, glancing down at her sweat covered body. She was certainly not equipped to deal with hot club goers at the moment. "Well, we could all get cleaned up first." Smack rolled her eyes, heading off her excuse. Smack seemed to read her mind sometimes. She leaned in, her voice taking on a conspiratorial tone. "Besides, I heard a rumor that they have a BDSM section there. It's pretty exclusive, but I bet I could get us in." She leaned back, looking pretty pleased with herself. Kisa only blinked at her, but all the other girls started talking rapidly, totally stoked to go.

"BDSM? Like, whips and chains? Why would we want to go in there?" Kisa was dumbfounded. They had nothing like that back home, and it was completely alien to her. Why would someone want to be hurt?

"It's more than that, K. Yeah, they have those things there, but it's all consensual. Besides, have you ever been spanked?" Smack fanned herself. "Good Lord, girl. You have no idea. It's like, the pain isn't pain. It just sets your nerve endings on fire. It consumes you, and you can't think of anything else. It's ah-maze-ing." She fake swooned into Helliot's lap. Helliot laughed and checked her pulse.

"You're a freak, Smack." Helliot chuckled. Smack just wagged her eyebrows at her.

"We're all freaks, darlin'. That's why we get along so well!" She blew her a kiss as she got up, grabbing her derby bag. "Who's in?" Most of the girls were in, all about letting their freak flags fly. They were so brave, while Kisa was just... not.

"I have a march to go to in the morning, so I'm out." They all groaned at Slam's words. She was their local protester, always fighting the good fight. Kisa actually really respected the strength of her convictions and her passion.

"Blah. Fine. K?" They all looked at Kisa. She appreciated always being invited, even though she continuously declined.

"Maybe next time?" Kisa hoped she sounded apologetic. The truth was, Kisa could only keep up her facade for so long. On the days she worked and had practice, she was completely wrecked by the end of the day. She just needed to be behind closed doors, in the silence, and allow that silence to consume her for a while. It was like she was a battery, and if she didn't get that time to recharge, she would die in the middle of rush hour. She knew what she could handle, and what she couldn't. Partying it up until dawn with these hooligans at some swingers' bar was not on the list of handleable things. She had a system. If she stuck to that system, she could survive. One day at a time.

"Sure, K. No biggie." Smack smiled, and Kisa again felt the swell of love for her teammates. Anyone else would have written off her loner ass long ago, but not these guys. They were all so unique, so different, and so accepting. It was the closest thing to a family she had ever had.

Kisa swallowed the lump in her throat, grabbed her bag, and followed them out.

She waited for Slam to lock up the rink, watching her set the alarm. She never wanted to leave her to lock up all alone, even though it was a pretty safe part of town. She felt protective of her girls. They walked to their cars, and after an invite to tie herself to a tree in the morning and a swift decline, Kisa was in the shelter of her maroon Honda Civic.

Feelings swelled within her. Emotions that she had shoved back all day boiled beneath her skin. Fuck. Why couldn't she just be normal? Why couldn't she grieve and move on, like she had convinced her parents she had? Why was she so broken? She started the car and headed home, refusing to give in to the tears. Deep breaths. Find three things, focus on them. She went through all the anxiety tricks she had learned through the grief counseling she had briefly gone to, trying to convince her parents not to admit her to a psych ward. It had been nearly impossible for her to function after Adam died, and she understood why her parents had drawn the line. From an outsider's perspective, she must have seemed a bit crazy. For her, though, she was anything but. It was a rational reaction to losing a piece of your soul. No, don't think about it. Deflect. Adjust.

She pulled into her apartment's parking garage, her knuckles white as they gripped the steering wheel. She couldn't breathe. Without taking out her derby bag, she hopped out of her beat up car. Her eyes were wild as she began to run. She didn't stop to lock her vehicle. She didn't stop at the alarmed look of the residents walking through the parking lot. She just ran. The physical exertion, the mind numbing exhaustion brought on by working out had been the only thing to save her this past year. Her legs burned, weakened from the two hours of practice she had just finished, but she pushed through it.

She could still see Adam. Could still feel him running his fingers through her hair. Could still hear his laugh as they watched cheesy Netflix comedies together. He always laughed so freely, never holding back. When was the last time she had truly laughed? She pushed harder, sweat rolling down her neck and adding to the already drenched jersey she wore. Thoughts of Adam tackling her in the weeds, tickling her endlessly, the both of them staring up at the blue skies. She wanted to scream.

The endless ache in her chest was getting worse. She had been trying to ignore it like everything else, but it was growing. She sometimes worried she had broken a rib in the accident and they had never caught it, the broken pieces scraping against her lungs. She couldn't breathe. Kisa doubled over, dry heaving.

She braced a shaking hand against the brick wall beside her, looking up and realizing she was at Abe's. She had run that far? She had been blindly running with no destination in mind, only escape from her inner demons. Trying to run from something inside of her seemed a bit pointless.

Trembling with fatigue, she walked to the front and glanced in the window. Abe was open at night, but the lights were dim tonight as if he had actually closed for once. She could see his bulletin board, covered with numerous flyers. One flyer in particular caught her attention. A large, black poster with crimson writing.

There is no Rest for the Wicked. Join us.
Restless

No other words or pictures were on the poster. She wouldn't even know what it advertised if not for the discussion at the rink earlier. Kisa shook her head, trying to clear it. She wanted to reach out and trace her fingers over the blood red letters. She made a fist, turning around and heading back towards her apartment. The entire walk back, Adam's fingers flitted through her hair and his chuckle danced against her ears.

Chapter Six

A scream echoed through Kisa's apartment. She looked around frantically, trying to see who the hell was screaming in her apartment at this time of night. Oh, she was. The scream abruptly halted at her realization. She was breathing rapidly, unable to pull in enough air. That tightness in her chest had her reaching up to rub her sternum. What had she been dreaming about? The nightmares were getting worse, the only blessing being that she very rarely remembered them. Sighing, she headed to the bathroom. Leaning over the sink, Kisa splashed cool water on her face, wiping away the sweat that clung to her. She stared at the depressing dark circles swallowing her eyes and wondered how much longer she could keep up this ruse.

With no hope for sleep, Kisa headed out to the kitchen, grabbing a bottle of water from the case that sat beneath her tiny kitchen table. Drinking deeply, Kisa plopped down with a sigh. She was exhausted, and the numbness was beginning to creep in again. She wasn't sure what was worse, the lung seizing panic attacks or the stretches of utter numbness where she felt nothing at all.

Pushing back the hair that had escaped her ponytail, she surveyed her quiet apartment. Grabbing her laptop, she opened up a Google tab. Unsure of what exactly she was doing, Kisa typed *Restless* into the search bar. Finding the website for the club, she gnawed on her chapped lip, debating for a moment before clicking on the link. Maybe the dream had left her feeling dramatic, but she couldn't help but feel that by clicking those tiny letters she was standing on a precipice. There were some moments, Kisa thought, that strike you as important, even when your mind can't connect why your body is reacting in such a way. Her palms felt sweaty, and she rolled her eyes at her own absurdity. She wasn't some small town girl anymore, afraid of big city clubs.

As the webpage filled her computer screen, she felt a twinge of disappointment. It was just a simple black page with the same red lettering she had seen on the flyer describing the location and club times. Frowning, Kisa scrolled down, assuming there had to be more. There was a small white rose in the bottom corner, and by instinct, Kisa clicked on it. Another tab opened and email addresses scrawled across the screen. What the heck? Were these the mods of the webpage? She tilted her head, curiosity burning through her. Randomly, she selected one of the email addresses. GHelic333. The new message box popped up in her email, and she debated about what to say. What was she looking for exactly? Deciding on simplicity, she wrote:

Hello, are you a member of the club? Could you tell me more about it?

Thanks- Kisa.

Chewing on a fingernail, she hit send. Closing the laptop, she got up and paced to the window. Looking out over the city, she envied all the dark lights, the residents probably sleeping peacefully, blissfully ignorant of their vulnerable existences. She leaned her head against the cool glass, closing her eyes. No, she didn't begrudge them their peace. She simply wished she could have a slice of it, hell, even a crumb would do. A ping sounded and she opened her eyes, her brows furrowing as she turned back towards her bedroom. She walked to her dresser and grabbed her phone. One new message blinked back at her. Already?

Heart racing, she hurried to her laptop, opening up her email once more.

Dearest Kisa,

Yes, I am a member of this organization. What may I help you to learn? I am a very good teacher. ;)

Yours truly,

Master G.

Kisa's face scrunched up. G sounded like a douche. Sighing, she debated about emailing someone else. Who else would respond at this hour? She needed the distraction. Opening her messenger app, she plugged in his address and requested to chat. Her knee bounced as she saw him accept. Well, now what, genius?

Kisa: Hi.

She groaned. Hi. So, she wasn't very poetic at 4 am. Sue her.

G: Hello dear.

Was this a seventy-year-old grandma?

Kisa: :) Can you tell me about the other aspects to the club?

G: Curiosity killed the cat, you know. ;)

If this guy sent her one more winky face...

Kisa: Ha. Well, we all die in the end, right?

Ugh. Could she be any more morbid? Was emo even a thing anymore?

G: Perhaps... Could we meet? It would be much easier to show you in person. Much more fun as well. ;)

Oh. My. Muthafuck. Another winky face...

Kisa: Not sure I am quite ready for that. Maybe you could just tell me a bit first?

G: Of course my dear. Well, it's a pretty typical BDSM club. Better than most, because I am there. What is your type?

Huh? Kisa was lost. What was her type? As in what did she look for in a man?

Kisa: Not sure yet.

G: Ah, new blood. Don't worry, I am sure we can figure that out. Tell me, Kisa darling, do you have a taste for pain? The escape it brings? The high that comes with it?

Kisa winced. Pain? Did she really want to go there with this asshat? She thought of the rush from derby, the thrill and adrenaline. Smack seemed to think it was the greatest high on earth. Kisa would never do drugs, not with her father's addictions constantly haunting her. Maybe this was another option? A way out from the numbness clenching around her heart.

G: Scared little one? Perhaps some incentive.

A request to view a webcam popped onto her laptop screen. Good gravy, if she clicked on this and a penis popped up, she was so done. There was no request to share her camera, which she saw as a bonus. She clicked okay and was pleasantly surprised when a face popped up on screen. Not a penis.

He was attractive, blonde hair curling around a chiseled face. Startling blue eyes looked back at her, a kind smile curving sensual lips.

Kisa: How do I know that's really you?

His eyes glanced down, reading her message. He tilted his head and then typed back.

G: Give me a sentence. Any sentence.

Kisa's mind was blank. A sentence. Surely she knew a sentence?

Kisa: To be or not to be?

He smiled, then grabbed something off screen. He was writing, and then he held up a piece of paper with her words written in elegant script. Smirking, he typed.

G: Satisfied my dear?

She cringed at the endearment. Something about this guy had her teeth on edge.

Kisa: Yes, thank you.

G: So, would you like to go to the club with me? I could introduce you to a whole new world, little pet.

Kisa thought for sure her eyes would fall out they rolled so hard.

Kisa: What exactly would going to the club entail?

G: Whatever you wanted it to. I am a Master though, not a submissive. I would require you to respect that role if you were to play with me.

Did he seriously just capitalize master? Sighing, Kisa thought about her options. Maybe she could use him to get into the club and then ditch him? She could explore more on her own. Maybe she could find someone less cringy to play with…

Kisa: Play how?

G: Well, there are many ways we could play. What are you most interested in?

What was she interested in? Kisa didn't feel very submissive. She certainly wasn't into some of the BDSM things she had googled. Seriously, vacuum bags? She got claustrophobic just thinking about it. One thing had stood out to her, and it was all she could currently think about.

Kisa: Pain.

G's eyes sparkled on the camera.

G: Lucky girl. Pain is my specialty. What are you doing tomorrow night?

Kisa was off the next day. She knew it, but she hesitated. Was she seriously considering this? This man could be a serial killer for all she knew. Swallowing, she stepped over that ledge. What did she have to lose at this point? She wasn't alive anymore, anyway.

Kisa: I'm free. Can we meet there?

He frowned, looking a little put off.

G: Don't you want to play somewhere more private?

Yep. He was definitely a serial killer.

Kisa: I would prefer we meet in public for the first time, for safety purposes. You understand.

He smiled, radiating patience. Oh, please.

G: Oh, of course my dear. Whatever makes you most comfortable. I will meet you there at 8, and we will explore this pain fetish of yours. Can you send me a picture so that I know who I am looking for?

Kisa stood up, running to the bathroom and looking at her appearance. Wincing slightly, she shrugged and grabbed her phone, snapping a quick picture and uploading it to her messenger. If he dropped her like a sack of potatoes, she would simply email someone else. She kind of hoped he did…

G: You are so beautiful. I can't wait to see you in person. XOXO

Kisa snorted. There was no way he really thought that. He was a terrible smooth talker. Although, with a face like that, she imagined he didn't have too much practice with the whole talking thing. Kisa bit her lip and then decided to send another message.

Kisa: Just so there isn't any confusion, I am not looking for sex. Only pain.

G's face grew cocky, and she could almost hear the scoff through the monitor as if no one could refuse him.

G: Whatever you say, pet. 8pm. Don't be late.

Kisa promptly shut her laptop, wondering what the hell she had just gotten herself into.

Chapter Seven

Dolor sat, his eyes closed, his head resting against the back of the crimson leather seat behind him. His eyes darted back and forth behind his lids, the music thudding through his veins. He was exhausted. Dolor didn't need to sleep, but at the moment, he ached for the rest that came from a deep slumber. He needed to feed, and soon. It had been too long, and he could feel his energy waning. His senses prowled through the club, spreading among the horde like a drop of blood in water. Seeking... tasting. The typical pain of loneliness, shame, and rejection were dispersed throughout. Tired hands clung to cold bottles and half-empty glasses, the liquor in them sloshing side to side in time with the music.

Reaching up and running his fingers through his thick hair, Dolor sighed. Shallow, their pain was shallow and unexciting. These humans created this pain with their mediocrity, their pathetic existences continuing through the cycles of meaningless sex, alcohol, and soulless careers. They loved material objects and then despaired when the love of another being eluded them. They were pawns, and they hadn't the desire to become kings. Satisfied in their dissatisfaction, they merely... existed. A sneer tugged onto his full lips. Why was this affecting him now? He had dealt with humans and their self-destructive behaviors for millennia.

Suddenly, a new taste caressed his tongue, settling in the back of his throat. His dark brows furrowed and he tilted his head to the side, a burning curiosity thrumming through him. Interesting... He felt as if he knew this scent, and yet he couldn't place the despair. He opened his eyes, the club lights reflecting off their depths. Those nebulous orbs scanned the crowd, scouring the shadows for that taunting aroma. His gaze slid to the back, the mass of people writhing on the dance floor obscuring his view. The black velvet curtain swayed softly, as if recently jostled.

Picking up his glass, Dolor threw the remnants of the rich bourbon into his mouth, enjoying the burn as he swallowed. "I'll see you later," he murmured to his companions as he rose, setting his now empty glass onto the round table. Mattheus chuckled, giving Dolor a knowing smirk. He recognized that predatory glint, as he had seen it many a time. Mattheus nodded, going back to his conversation.

Dolor stalked across the dance floor, hands reaching for him, trailing across his black suit jacket, their pain sending tingles across his skin. His hunger rolled, building within him. Later, he told that hunger, shoving it back forcefully. He arrived at the swinging fabric, his long fingers caressing it gently. A dark smile pulled at him. How many nights did he end up behind the veil? Too many. This pain…this pain he had a taste for and his pulse quickened in anticipation.

Dolor pushed aside the curtain, stepping into the dark hallway beyond. A single red bulb hung halfway down the hall, the glow creating a sinister feel. Theatrics, as if those who entered here needed them. He had seen the abyss they sought; had helped them soar into its loving embrace, and never once had he needed any damn theatrics. The hallway was quiet, the thick walls and curtain muffling the sounds that lay ahead and the booming music behind him.

A man stood in front of the wooden door at the end of the hall, his hulking form looming, daring anyone to approach. Though not actually a man, he was a leshy, a guardian of the forest. Dolor, not a short man himself, had to arch his neck back to stare into the face of the leshy.

Nearly seven feet tall, he stood in a crisp and notably expensive black suit. His tie was a deep green, reflecting the green of his eyes. His hair was cut short, but not short enough to hide that it was indeed green as well, the mossy curls lying close to his scalp.

A fearsome creature, the leshy had been working for Mattheus at the club now for about five years. He was a loyal employee, paying back a debt to Dolor's business partner. What that debt was, Dolor did not know. Curious, he had asked the leshy and Mattheus on multiple occasions about the debt, but they had remained tight-lipped. None of the other regulars seemed to be any more knowledgeable about the arrangement than he was. Dolor nodded, smiling up at the man. "Busy night, Charles?"

Charles' chuckle made Dolor's bones ache. Ancient and deep, his voice was the rumble of trees falling, crawling out of that thick throat. "You could say that, D. How about you? Haven't seen you in a while."

Dolor shrugged, picking at his cufflinks. "I was out of town for a bit, and the scene has been dull as of late."

Charles nodded, his jaw tightening. Dolor immediately noticed the grinding of teeth, and his curiosity spiked. "Is there something the matter, Charles?"

This time it was Charles' turn to shrug. "Not my club, not my decisions."

Dolor's brows furrowed. "Meaning?"

His massive jaw tightened further. "Gideon is back."

At that, Dolor's eyes narrowed. "Mattheus approved of this?" Charles nodded, a man of few words. Dolor felt his fingers clench, wondering about this turn of events. "Are the DM's aware?"

Charles nodded once more. "I told them all to be on high alert and to not allow him access to the private rooms." Dolor nodded in approval. If Mattheus had allowed this, he had just cause. He was many things, but foolish was not one of them.

"Very well. If things escalate again, perhaps I shall handle the situation personally." A wicked smile curved Dolor's lips, and he felt that hunger swell. Charles chuckled again, shaking his head.

"Even Gideon isn't that stupid." His low timbre rumbled, stepping aside to allow Dolor to pass.

"Too bad…" Dolor sighed as he moved to the wooden door, slipping inside and shutting it behind him.

The room was dark, the bulbs casting a red haze on the creatures congregating beneath them. The flashing white of the strobe lights slid across their sweat coated skin as they moved to the harsh music pounding from the speakers. The ceiling was tall and long midnight curtains draped down from the rafters, lining the walls and creating a sort of barrier to section off the massive room.

Dolor allowed his eyes to adjust, the sounds sinking into his bones and making his muscles both relax and tighten at the same time. He eyed the different sections, noting the humans and non-humans mingled together. He closed his eyes, focusing on the scent that had lured him there. Blood, lust, pain, fear. Too many scents clouded his mind and he shook his head, trying to focus. He needed another drink.

He looked up, noticing Joro leaning her back against the bar, her slanted black eyes gazing out at the crowd. He headed over to her, nodding at the bartender who nodded back and got him his usual concoction. She was wearing red tonight, the tight form-fitting corset leaving little to the imagination. She smiled tightly at him, the only acknowledgement she gave before her attention went back to the floor.

Rage prickled Dolor's nose as he sidled up to her, sitting on the stool beside her. He tracked her glare, tensing at the golden head weaving through the crowd. His nostrils flared, and his fingers tightened on his glass. Gideon. Glancing back up, he watched Joro's lip lift in a silent snarl. Her black leather gloves rested behind her on the bar, and he winced as her nails pierced through them, slicing into the expensive wood.

"Easy, J," he murmured, chuckling softly.

Her furious stare snapped down to his. The light reflected off her multifaceted eyes, the many sides glowing eerily. They were large eyes for her small, heart shaped face, the slight angle doing nothing to ease their peculiarity. They hinted at the secrets that lay beneath her skin, and Dolor wondered not for the first time why she didn't simply glamor them too. Perhaps she enjoyed the fear they induced. One didn't stare into her soul lightly.

"Why is he back here, Dolor? Does Mattheus know?" Her words shook with rage, but Dolor tasted the pain that threaded them.

Joro didn't often allow her emotions to get the better of her and had one of the best shields Dolor had come across. What Gideon had done to her had truly unsettled her. His jaw ticked. He had nearly killed the demon for it, but Mattheus had intervened. The betrayal of that intervention still haunted Joro's eyes, and the walls that had begun to fall between them all were cool steel once more. She wouldn't trust again so easily. It made Dolor sigh. He had few true friends in this world, but he thought of Joro as one of them.

"Yes, I know," Mattheus answered, sidling up to the bar, his voice deceptively light. He had ditched his current arm candy and instead held two wine glasses, one of which he handed to J. A peace offering. His green eyes begged her to accept the glass, and she did, but not before she drew those sharp claws across the bar tabletop. The sound made Mattheus wince and the sickly sweet smile she gave him caused him to wisely hold his tongue. He was vastly protective of his bar, and the fact he said nothing about the deep gouges showed how desperate he was for her forgiveness.

"Gideon's father made a bargain with me. If we gave Gideon a pass on the... insult he gave you, he would open trade to the mines. Everyone has been trying to get access to the minerals there for millennia, and it opens up revenue for the entire Helic region." He sighed, looking tired as he slid gracefully onto a stool. "It is in the contract that if Gideon breaks code one more time, his father will handle the matter personally. What do you suppose the odds are of that bastard following the rules? I didn't give him a pass, J. I simply extended his death sentence." The tension eased slightly from Joro's shoulders, and Mattheus gave her a lopsided grin.

She nodded once at him, and then swayed into the crowd, off to find a new fly for her web no doubt. Dolor looked over at Mattheus, watching his hungry gaze linger on J's backside. He chuckled. That dance had been going on for quite some time, and Dolor had an internal bet on who would stumble first. His bet was on Mattheus. Mattheus cleared his throat, shifting on the stool.

"So, the Helic region? That's a hell of a piece of the pie. Are you sure we're ready for such a trade?" Dolor asked, continuing to scan the crowd. Where was she? His knee began to bounce, the instinct to hunt itching to take over.

"Someone is going to open that trade eventually, and it

might as well be us. We have open portals in nearly every realm available through you. We can offer the most product across the most ground. Helix knows this, which is why he offered the bargain in the first place. He also knows his son is a ticking time bomb. Without this outlet, Helix fears where Gideon will put that pent up rage. It's leverage we need right now. Think, Dolor. This will make us one of the top trading lines in all realms. We should be celebrating!" Mattheus nodded to the bartender and several shots appeared, along with several scantily clad women. "Body shots! Body shots for everyone!"

The crowd cheered and Dolor rolled his eyes. Sometimes he thought Mattheus had been body snatched by a college drop out.

Dolor removed himself from the over excess of giggling and salt and worked his way through the crowd. He found Gideon in a corner, circling a woman strapped to the St. Andrews cross. Dolor crossed his arms, leaning against a beam and watching the scene. The woman had her back to Gideon, her chest resting against the cross, arms stretched above her and legs spread. Each limb was strapped to the corners of the cross with elaborate cuffs, and her chestnut hair hung between the front of her face and the wood, hiding her face from view. She was in black, boy short styled underwear and a simple black tank top. Dolor frowned. Normally the women who came to the club fancied themselves up a bit. Nudity wasn't allowed, so they made it a game to get as close to it as possible. Thongs and black duct tape across nipples, never tank tops.

Dolor sniffed and felt his entire body freeze. She was human, and she was also the prey he had been searching for. The pain that radiated off her had Dolor's pupils dilating. His mouth opened slightly, and he licked his lips at the taste. He couldn't think for a moment, and then all of his thoughts came rushing back to him at once. Why was Gideon playing with a human? Who was she? What was this pain she held? He couldn't place it, and that was something that never happened. Dolor knew all forms of pain.

He shifted and moved closer, knowing they had just begun their scene. Gideon was drawing back a wicked looking belt, bringing it down across the woman's creamy thighs. She was fit, her muscles toned and sleek. The welt was instant, the red standing out harshly even in the dim lighting. She didn't move. Not even a flinch. Had he already warmed her up? No, there were no other marks on her. Dolor felt his teeth grind. Of course, Gideon wouldn't give a warm up. He wasn't in it for the submissives' enjoyment, what did he care about getting them into the proper headspace? The sharp crack of the belt sounded again, another welt joining the other. No sound, no reaction.

Dolor moved closer still, noting the shock on Gideon's face. Gideon loved tears and screams. It was his fix, and from the rage melting his normally handsome features, Dolor could tell the silence had been unexpected. Dolor smirked. That a girl. He felt a strange swell of pride in her silence. She was strong, and wouldn't break that easily. Gideon seemed to have come to the same conclusion, as he threw down the belt, rifling through his trunk of toys. He pulled out a cat-o'-nine-tails, the barbs glistening in the light.

Dolor tensed and felt a familiar stirring within his chest. His beast stretched, filling his skin and looking out through his eyes. *She is ours. Ours to hurt. Ours to eat.* His beast growled, and Dolor felt his own lip curl. Gideon gripped the woman's thick locks and jerked her head back roughly. Dolor felt his heart stop at the first glimpse of her face. She was smiling. No, she was laughing. Full belly, shoulders shaking, tears rolling kind of laughter echoed across the room.

She was the most beautifully broken creature he had ever seen.

Gideon's face turned red, his eyes flashing to crimson as his glamor faltered. Rookie. Dolor shook his head at the display. Gideon leaned over, whispering something into the woman's ear. Her laughter stopped abruptly, her face pale and her eyes widening in fear. It made him want to rip the man's tongue out and feed it to the hounds. Suddenly, Gideon gripped the tank top, ripping it down the middle. The woman inhaled sharply and began to squirm, clearly uncomfortable with the exposure.

Dolor worked his way closer, ready to stop this charade at the first utterance of a safe word. He was nearly there when Gideon reached his arm back, bringing down the barbed flogger with supernatural force across the woman's exposed back. Her head arched back and a ragged gasp escaped her throat, but she didn't scream. Somehow, she held it in. One moment Dolor was in the crowd, the next he was before Gideon. He stared at the man, his hands in his pockets, a wicked smile begging Gideon to do something. Anything. All he needed was one excuse to rip him to fucking shreds. Gideon visibly startled at his abrupt appearance, wiping away the sweat that had begun running down his face.

"She... She hasn't safe worded. Get out of my way." He straightened his shoulders, trying to act as if he didn't saturate the air around them with his fear. Dolor looked back at the woman. Gently, he ran his finger along her spine, drawing another gasp from her. He brought the finger forward, showing Gideon the blood there. Dolor tutted, shaking his head at the young demon as he sucked the bloody fingertip into his mouth. He knew the rules, and the rage that slid across his handsome features made Dolor's smile grow. No bloodletting allowed.

Without another word, Gideon shoved his tools back into his case, not even cleaning them. What a walking health code violation. Gideon didn't remove the woman's bonds, didn't utter a word as he stormed through the crowd.

"Fucking ass," Dolor mumbled, walking to the woman's front. He tried looking up through that curtain of hair, but there was nothing for it. Shaking his head, he decided to do what he had ached to from the moment he saw her. He moved her hair back from her face. "You alright, kitten?" As her eyes met his, Dolor took a step back. They were bottomless, the pain there offering him a home. All he had to do was step into them, and it could all be over. They offered him not death, but complete nothingness. The end of his very essence. Then, they were just normal, pretty, brown eyes. Not the pit of all despair, just eyes. Had he imagined that?

Her words were full of that pain and rage as she slung them at him. "I'm not your fucking kitten."

With that, the Dungeon Masters in charge of monitoring the scenes released her wrists and she stumbled from the cross. She grabbed her coat from the floor, throwing it on with a wince and searching for her pants. Dolor knew he should reach for her, help her, eat her, fuck her... Anything but just stand there like an imbecile.

He looked down at his feet, startled to see they hadn't moved. He was frozen in place, and Dolor felt something he had only felt one other time in his long, lonely existence. Fear. For the first time, Dolor let his prey escape, and wondered if perhaps she wasn't prey, but predator.

Chapter Eight

Three days. It took Kisa three days to lose the adrenaline and shock coursing through her system. Three days for the numbness to crawl its way back up her throat. Three days for the wounds on her body to disappear, leaving only the wounds on her soul for her to focus on.

Closing her eyes, she rested her head back on the seat. Her car was cold, the radio silent, but she didn't have the energy to reach out and turn on the heat. Worse. It was so much worse today. She had gotten a taste, and damn her if she didn't want another. For a few brief moments, Kisa had forgotten Adam. She had forgotten the mind-consuming grief. She had forgotten the silent screaming in her spirit. There had been no numbness on that cross. There had been nothing but her. Her body. Her will. Her strength.

It was strange, but Kisa had never felt more powerful than when she was strapped to that cross. After everything she had been through, the physical pain had been nothing.

Had it been nothing, though? No, it had been everything. It had been a reprieve from the misery she had become accustomed to.

Until that twat had taunted her. He threatened to rape her right in the middle of the club. Told her no one would stop him. It had quickly torn her from her happy place of pain and into one of fear. What had she been thinking? Things could have gone so wrong. Not again. She wouldn't make any more reckless decisions like that, no matter how much she craved to feel that brief respite in her despair.

The sound of a door had Kisa opening her eyes. She glanced at the clock on the dash. There were still ten minutes left until her father's meeting wrapped up. Her head lolled lazily to the side, out of instinct more than curiosity. Her curious nature couldn't break through the wall of numbness erected around her essence.

A man had exited the building, leaning his tall frame against the side of the brick wall. Broad shoulders were covered in a sharp, black suit that tapered down to a narrow waist. No wrinkles in sight. Kisa glanced down at her own wrinkled scrubs and squirmed in her seat. She had just worked a twelve-hour shift, after all. Glancing back up, she tried to see the man's face, but his dark hair had swung forward to shield it as he searched through his pockets. Suddenly, his head snapped up and his eyes locked with hers. Kisa felt her heart stutter and then stop all together.

His eyes, even in the dark and across the parking lot, shone. It was as if he had captured the stars and shoved them into the blackness of his pupils. They sucked her in, and when Kisa finally breathed again it was a jagged breath, full of wonder. His eyes hooded with interest and he began to stalk towards her. This man didn't merely walk. Oh no, that was definitely a stalking gait. She turned away, her heart seeming to have decided it needed to make up for its temporary lapse by beating in double time. She swallowed thickly, looking anywhere but out towards the sexy behemoth strutting towards her. So, naturally, she jumped when there was a gentle tap on her window. Closing her eyes, she attempted to collect herself before looking up.

He was leaning down, a sexy smirk gracing his movie star lips. It had been so long since Kisa had felt any sort of attraction towards someone. She stared, and knew she was staring, and couldn't look away. His eyes were not stars and shadows now, but still just as stunning. Up close, she could see they were actually the deepest blue she had ever seen. As if when God created him, he originally made those stunning eyes black, then realized black wasn't normally an eye color so he dropped the barest hint of blue to them. He stared back, that dark gaze seeming to devour her whole. He tapped the glass again, looking down, clearly suggesting she should lower it. Should she? She wasn't exactly in the best part of town. She glanced again at his fancy suit and around at her ancient car, wondered what a man like that could possibly want to steal from her, and lowered the window.

"Hello again."

She startled slightly. His voice. Good gravy that voice. It was all chocolate and sin wrapped in velvet. She shivered as she felt that voice trace dark circles down her skin. Wait, again? Her brows bunched in confusion. She would never have forgotten that face.

"I... I'm sorry?" she responded, embarrassed at the husky tone that emerged. Get it together, Kisa, she thought furiously. He looked just as confused as she did, clearly surprised she didn't remember him.

"You don't remember me?" He sounded a bit shocked. Most likely this tall hunk of man was not used to being forgotten so easily. "We met at the club the other night?"

Kisa's mind raced. What club? She never went clubbing. He must have her mixed up with someone else. Surely, he couldn't mean...

"You were at Restless, right?" He smiled again, and she tried to think between her heart's stutter. She should probably get that checked out.

She turned her face, red racing up her neck and flushing her cheeks. Of course, why had she thought people wouldn't recognize her outside of the club? She hadn't even considered the possibility. Stupid. She had been so stupid to do that in such a public place.

"I'm afraid you must have me confused with someone else," she mumbled, her palms sweating. This walking sex on a stick had seen her practically naked.

"You're a bit hard to forget, kitten," he purred, his finger tracing down her heated cheek. Her eyes snapped back to his, fury mixing with her embarrassment. She remembered him now. He was the reason her night had been cut off early. She had been in such a distracted, adrenaline-fused haze that she hadn't even registered the details of his face.

"Don't call me that," she heard herself snap.

His eyes widened in amusement. He tilted his head, leaning closer. "I suppose you had better give me your name then." Suddenly, his scent hit her through the window. It was like a physical slap. If his voice had affected her, it was nothing compared to his smell. He smelled like clear skies, old books, and warm cookies. He smelled like home. How could someone smell like all of those things at once?

She caught herself leaning towards him, trying to take in more of that scent, and jerked back abruptly. He was watching her closely as if analyzing her every reaction.

"I don't see why that's relevant." She turned away again, glancing at the clock. Seven minutes. Only three minutes had gone by. Had time slowed down? Maybe her dad would come out early. This man was dangerous, and she needed to get away from him before she made even a bigger fool of herself.

"Well, it is part of a normal introduction." He stood, extending his hand. Large hands. Kisa swallowed and nearly giggled at the thought. This man had clearly kicked her brain back to her teenage years. "My name is Dolor. And you are?"

She stared at that outstretched hand. If his voice and smell affected her so, his touch might just make her spontaneously combust. She didn't really want to die today.

"I'm not interested," she said shakily, looking away from him again. Five minutes. She could stay strong for five minutes. Yeah. Of course.

"Hmm. I'm pretty good at reading people, and I was definitely getting an interested vibe." He placed both his hands on the roof of the car and leaned down towards her. More of that scent moved through the car and she found her eyes trailing up his lean body to the smug face attached to it.

"Does the over confident thing normally work for you?" she asked icily, steeling her face as she looked back into those stunning eyes. His eyes sparkled and he shrugged.

"I do alright, kitten." He was back to smirking. Kisa wanted to smack it off his stupid, pretty face. Or kiss it.

Looking back towards the meeting door, Kisa silently prayed for her father to hurry up. Her eyes snapped back to the infuriating stranger. "Look, I am sure you're a swell guy, but I am really not interested. I have enough complication in my life without adding a..." she paused, slowly evaluating his appearance before taking a guess, "gambling addict?"

"You have a problem with addicts, kitten?"

"Stop calling me that. And no, I don't. I just don't need the complications that come with one. So..." She waited for him to turn away, but he simply looked at her with those unnerving eyes and stupidly delicious smirk.

"Well, I assure you I am not a gambling addict. I am writing a paper for the medical society about the epidemic in this town." His face had turned serious, and she paused. She had been trying to get someone to do more outreach about the heroin epidemic for years. Unfortunately, no one wanted to be involved until crimes had been committed, or some poor soul had overdosed.

"Medical society? Are you investigating the doctors nearby then?"

He eyed her scrubs, his brow lifting sardonically.

"No one you know, I hope. It is more a general assessment about the causes and outcomes."

"Oh. Well, good. Someone needs to shine a light on the assholes overprescribing around here." Kisa stopped the tirade she could feel boiling within her. It made her so angry to hear the stories, the heartbroken loved ones, the overdoses that came into the emergency room. It was something that Adam and she had planned on tackling as a team. They were going to form a committee and try to educate the public more. They had lain together late into the night on many occasions discussing the ways they could make change in that community. She swallowed painfully, looking back at the clock. Two minutes.

"Maybe I could pick your brain sometime over coffee?" He looked so sincere looking down at her. He was incredibly handsome, and he seemed not to be entirely heartless. Kisa chewed her lip, debating.

"Hey, Dolor. I see you met my daughter, Kisa?"

Kisa groaned and dropped her head back again. Her father had the worst habit of saying the wrong things.

"Kisa…" Dolor purred. She glared at him, surprised at the huge smile encompassing his face. "Yes, Kisa and I were just getting acquainted." His eyes danced as they drank her in. She felt herself blushing again, and turned to her dad as he got into the car.

"Ready?" she said, trying to ignore the heat pouring

through the window beside her. Her father looked from Dolor back to her, nodding and scrunching his eyes in confusion.

"I'll see you around, Kisa," Dolor said, leaning back away from the car. She felt a pang of disappointment as his scent retreated with him.

"Not likely," she murmured before pulling away, refusing to look in the rearview mirror as she left him behind. As she headed towards her dad's apartment, two things occurred to her. One, the numbness had receded, replaced by irritation and lust. Two, she had forgotten to take her work badge off, and her name had been on display for him the entire time.

Chapter Nine

Dolor was totally fucked. He could not get Kisa out of his head. It was distracting him from every aspect of his life. He had been so stunned by his reaction to her at the club that he had sworn to let it lie. He didn't need complicated in his life right now, especially with the Helic region opening up for trade. He needed to be focused. He had convinced himself to let her and her dark chasm eyes go. After he saw her at that meeting though, he knew, without a shadow of a doubt, that he had to have her. The passion that had flickered in her eyes had intrigued him to no end.

He had never before been interested in the dealings of mortals, and still was unsure of what had pushed him into going to the Narcotics Anonymous meetings in the first place. At first, he had reasoned it was an easy feed. Where else could you find such a gathering of pain? After listening to meeting after meeting of such a baring of souls, however, Dolor was unsure if he was lying to himself. He had begun writing the drug epidemic paper shortly thereafter.

The week had gone by in a blur, and he was grateful it was Friday. On top of the club and trade work, Dolor occasionally took on interesting cases as a surgeon, and he had thrown himself into that work this week. He had made a name for himself over time, giving him the opportunity to pick and choose the cases he wanted. He had originally gotten into the medical field for the easy access to pain, but as time went on he developed a thirst for the challenge. While he still occasionally worked in emergency surgery, he mostly selected the rare cases that no one else wanted, reveling in the victory of achieving results that most couldn't.

He knew from Kisa's badge that she worked at the same hospital as he, but no matter how frequently he searched for her, she never turned up. He was beginning to wonder if she had quit and he would never see her again. She worked in an entirely different section of the hospital from him, but he had been finding excuses to venture around, hoping to run into her. He shook his head. He was acting like a desperate schoolboy.

He needed to feed, that was all. His hunger was making him act irrationally. Every time he went to feed, however, nothing seemed appetizing. It was like shoving ashes into a starving man's face. He had tasted heaven in the few moments he sampled Kisa's exquisite pain, and he wanted more. He would find her, and he would convince her to give in to him. He licked his lips in anticipation.

"Dolor? Have you heard a word I've said?"

Irritated, he turned from the window and turned back into the incessant droning speech of the surgeon behind him rambling on about some new procedure, practically salivating at the prospect of Dolor assisting him with it. The man, Dr. Stevens, knew that without more funding and the name Dolor Comedenti on his dissertation, the dream of continuing his next big breakthrough would be finished. Dolor smiled inwardly. If only they knew the origins of that name.

He was finished with this conversation, or lack thereof. He had a kitten to find. "I will consider your proposal, Stevens. My secretary will be in touch." He smiled coolly, enjoying the tightening of the good doctor's shoulders. Titles... since the beginning of time they have had so much power. Power to show respect, and power to remove it.

Stevens nodded curtly, his lips pressed together in a hard line. He stood and offered his stubby, velvety hand. Surgeons treated their hands like crystal. A dark thought caressed Dolor's mind, like a lover, as he gazed at that outstretched palm. Crystal makes such a lovely sound when it shatters.

Dolor strode forward those few steps, grasping that fragile hand firmly into his own large, calloused palm. Flickers of pride, anger, and desperation danced across the doctor's features, even though he tried to hide his thoughts in an impassive mask. Dolor's hand squeezed tighter, watching the corners of Stevens' eyes crinkle and flinch. That pain slid across Dolor's tongue, enticing him, though it tasted of day old tobacco and gambling debts. Unappetizing. Without another word, Dolor turned back to the window, effectively dismissing the man.

He stared down at the people walking in and out of the cafeteria below. Decision made, Dolor grabbed his food from the refrigerator in his office, deciding to go and eat with the local rabble. Surely she had to eat? The cafeteria was the one place he hadn't looked. Dolor didn't have to eat usually, but with the lack of his typical feeding he needed, the energy. The less he ate off pain, the more physical nutrition he required. It was a nuisance, really. However, today he was hoping it would be his silver lining.

Dolor entered the cafeteria. His heart began to race as a familiar scent shot straight to his dick. He barely bit back the groan as his eyes searched the sea of scrubs. Startled brown eyes caught his, and he felt a wicked smile curve his lips. Got you…Like a startled rabbit, Kisa grabbed the book she had been reading and what remained of her apple and shot through the cafeteria, heading out the back door towards the rear garden. Dolor's smile grew, and he felt his beast stretch, ready for the chase. Bad move, kitten.

He followed her scent through the garden that weaved behind the campus. Large oaks shadowed the sidewalk, giving a reprieve from the chemical odors and steely aspect of the hospital. Following the sidewalk, he turned a corner and paused. Her smell was fading. Tilting his head, Dolor sniffed and backtracked. He walked around one wide tree trunk, and there she was, sitting with her back against the trunk and nearly hidden by a leafy bush nearby. Her cheeks flushed as she saw him. He smiled and watched her visibly swallow.

"There you are, kitten," he purred, enjoying the taste of her anger as it flared. It was laced with pain, and the bastard in him licked up the scraps. Her mental walls were almost as good as Joro's and he knew he would have to work for this feast. She wouldn't let him in easily. His beast relished the challenge.

"I've told you not to call me that." She glared at him, and he bowed dramatically.

"My apologies, Kisa. May I join you?" Before she could say no, he sat on the grass beside her. She looked startled and eyed his expensive pants warily. He had spare suits in his office, of course.

"You're gonna get all dirty," she muttered, the mother hen in her endearing. His smile grew into a mischievous grin, and her flush deepened as she realized what she had said. "That... That's not what I meant." She squirmed, and he delighted in her discomfort.

"Yes, well, getting a little dirty never hurt anyone." He leaned closer, his words sliding across her neck. He watched her swallow again and the scent of her arousal thickened the air. His nose trailed delicately behind her ear, smelling her. She shivered and gripped her book tighter.

"W-what do you want?" She licked her lips, seeming

unsure of where to look. Her eyes landed on another tree in front of her and stuck there. He smirked.

"You, of course." He leaned back, staring at her profile and willing her to look at him. She didn't. Frustrated, he grabbed her ponytail, tugging her head around to face him. She gasped at the slight pain, her mouth parted and her breath hitched. "Much better," he murmured as his eyes latched onto hers. She didn't pull away, but leaned closer to him, her focus darting towards his mouth. "Do you see something you want, Kisa?" He kept his fist in her hair, pulling gently. She closed her eyes, her breath coming out in a ragged rush.

"More..." she whispered. Dolor smiled victoriously, jerking her forward by her hair and tracing her lips with his tongue.

"Play with me, kitten," he whispered back, jerking her head to the side and nuzzling her throat. He wanted to roll on top of her, drown himself in the scent of her pain and lust. The sharp stab that flared every time he used that nickname of hers made him groan, and his cock strained against the front of his slacks. He leaned forward and bit her shoulder. Hard. She gasped and pressed her chest into him, her stiff nipples teasing him with their nearness. Why didn't he carry clamps on him at all times? She whimpered when his teeth finally let go of their hold. They were both breathing heavily, and he wondered if anyone would notice if he threw her down right there and fucked her among the trees. Looking into her hooded eyes, he thought she would be up for it. Maybe exhibition was in her bag of kinks? Who knew?

"Say yes," he murmured, pressing his thickness against her thigh, practically pulling her into his lap. Her eyes widened, and he watched her pulse thud in her pale throat.

"I-I don't want to have sex with you," she stuttered. He

smiled at her, noting how she pressed her thighs together, her dilated pupils, and the way she leaned even closer to him.

"You are a terrible liar, my dear." He smirked, leaning forward and nipping her lip playfully. A sharp flare of pain made Dolor's breath hitch. He leaned back quickly, his eyes locking on hers. Despair. Emptiness. Death. Pain. Nothingness. All of these things looked back at him and he quickly let go of her. Just as they had at the club, her black eyes beckoned him and terrified him. And just as suddenly as it had then, it disappeared. Dull brown eyes looked back at him, all of that lusty fire extinguished. What had just happened?

"I need to go." Kisa's voice was hollow, and he didn't stop her as she rose and straightened her scrubs. For the second time, he watched as his little predator ran away, too stunned to follow her.

Chapter Ten

"Daddy... Please, let's go..." Kisa felt her dad's calloused palm gently pull out of her grip. She watched in despair as he turned to head down the long hallway.

"It's okay, pumpkin. I'll just be a minute. Why don't you go play with Adam, hmm?" Before she could respond, he was gone. She closed her eyes tightly, trying to stop the tears from falling. What would she tell mama?

"Keep an eye on your dad. Keep him out of trouble, okay? Don't let him go anywhere he shouldn't," her mom had told her before they had left. She had failed miserably.

A gentle touch wiped a traitorous tear from her cheek. "Don't cry, kitten." The soft southern drawl made her smile. Adam.

"I wasn't crying," she grumbled as she wiped at her face.

"You're a terrible liar, darlin'." He smiled sympathetically. He was tall for his age, only a year older than her eleven. His messy blonde hair stuck up in every direction and his clothes looked like he had been wrestling in the mud. They had been friends for years, ever since Adam and his dad had moved there from Alabama. His dad... shared with her dad. It was always so bitter when they came here. The joy of seeing Adam mixed with her father's, and her, failure.

"Come on. I got somethin' to show ya." He grabbed her hand and led her out the trailer door. They passed a car up on blocks, heading around to the backyard. The summer sun beat down relentlessly, and Kisa was glad she wore shorts today instead of her usual blue jeans. Adam didn't release her hand, and she found the usual comfort in him.

"They don't mean it, ya know. Our folks, I mean. They have a disease. Saw it on Oprah, I did." His words made no sense to her, but Adam had always been the smart one. It would be easier to think her dad couldn't help himself. The smell of lilacs reached her nose and her eyes widened at the huge bush before them. It was the biggest she had ever seen, and she laughed. Adam had his shoulders back, looking oddly proud of his lilacs.

"That's as big as a house!" She giggled. He grinned, then tugged her towards a small trail that had been cut into the bush. "Did you do this?" The bush had a clear path cut into it, and they ducked down as they worked their way through it. He let go of her hand, having to hunch more than her with his extra height.

"Yep. Me and my da." The pride was evident as they wove deeper into the bush. The smell was almost overwhelming. Books and toys cluttered the trail, and she could see Adam hiding out in here, reading until dark. He was such a bookworm. His daddy got mean sometimes, and he told her he knew the best hiding places. She was touched he was showing them to her now.

The bush was getting thicker, and the sunlight wasn't shining as bright now. It was getting darker, and Kisa stumbled on a rock. She looked up, and Adam was further away from her.

"Adam! Adam, wait!" Stupid boys, always leaving her behind. She hurried to close the gap, but it just kept growing. She seemed to be getting caught on the branches as if they were reaching for her. She cried out as she fell again, a brutal thorn slicing into her arm. Lilacs don't have thorns…

As soon as she thought it, a branch shot out and wrapped around her throat. She grappled with it, trying to pry it off, trying to call for Adam or her daddy. Adam was nowhere in sight, and Kisa's eyes widened as something large snapped branches in the bush before her. It tore itself a path, and Kisa could do nothing but watch as the horror of the thing unfolded. The creature stood. Kisa began to sob. Ten feet tall, the monster had crimson skin, twinkling blue eyes, and an evil grin. He leaned towards her and dragged a black tongue up her cheek.

"Soon," its gravelly voice whispered to her.

With a scream, Kisa tore herself from the nightmare. She scrambled off the bed and into the bathroom. Crashing onto her knees, she barely made it to the toilet before losing what little dinner she had eaten. Resting her head on the porcelain, Kisa tried to calm her breathing, going through the usual techniques. It was just a dream. Just a weird dream. Finally, her breathing slowed. She rose on shaky legs, leaning over the sink to rinse her mouth. As she reached for the knob, her eyes landed on a wicked slash running down her arm. The blood stood out harshly in the fluorescent lighting, and Kisa wondered, not for the first time, if she was losing her mind.

Kisa was chewing her nails. She never chewed her nails. They were bitten to the quick, and she ran them through her messy hair. She was going insane. She constantly felt on edge, and she needed to release this ball of pent up energy. She gazed out of the bookstore window. She had been hanging out at Abe's a lot this week, for once not wanting to be alone. Practice had been cancelled due to a freak snowstorm, and the snow still covered the streets outside. She closed her eyes, hating the snow. The first winter without... Don't think about it, she told herself.

She stood, determined to find another book. She stopped abruptly, reaching up to smooth her hair. At the end of the narrow aisle, Dolor stood, book in hand. His eyes widened, clearly surprised at seeing her. Those eyes instantly turned hungry and he stalked closer. She swallowed, looking down self-consciously. She wore black leggings and a dark blue sweater that hung to her mid thighs. Sunday comfy, she called it. She licked her suddenly dry lips, eyes returning to his. He stopped before her, that smirk lighting up his face.

"Fancy seeing you here, kitten." His voice had the same effect it always had on her. She felt her body go soft, her breathing accelerate. Good gravy, this man's voice. "I didn't think anyone else knew about this place," he murmured, stepping closer. She backed up, jumping as she felt her back bump into one of the many bookshelves. He followed, setting his book on the shelf to her right. "Nervous, kitten?"

She lifted her chin, trying to sound like she wasn't planning her escape. "Hardly. And don't call me that."

He braced his hands on the shelves on either side of her head, his large form looming over her. He leaned down and his scent made her close her eyes. Now she knew where the old book smell came from. His nose slid up her neck. Was he smelling her?

"My apologies, Kisa. You seem to make me forget myself." His words were barely a whisper and goosebumps rose in their wake as they caressed her skin. "Have you thought about my offer?" He leaned back, looking into her eyes.

Oh, had she. Nearly every night. How could she not? Every time she had though, it had ended with his powerful body thrusting into her. She couldn't betray Adam that way. She couldn't risk it with this man. He was too tempting.

"I... I won't have sex with you. Why would you want to play with me?" Her heart raced. He watched her mouth like a starving man looking at a feast.

"There is fun to be had without sex, Kisa." He grinned, running his thumb along her bottom lip. Without thinking, she ran her tongue over where he had touched, and she had to restrain herself from moaning. The man tasted like sin. His eyes hooded with lust, and he leaned closer to her. "Shall I show you, kitten?"

Without warning, he gripped her shoulders and turned her around roughly. Her chest pressed into the books in front of her. He let go of her, only to grip her hip with one hand and put his other at the top of her spine. He jerked her hips back at the same time as he pushed her torso down. She gripped the bookshelf, bent in half before him, her gaze glancing out the window to her left for passersby. Her heart thundered and her panties had grown damp. Fuck. What was she doing?

"You say stop, and we stop. Understood?" His words were firm, and Kisa couldn't help but rub her thighs together, craving friction. He had said no sex. She jerked as a firm slap landed on her backside. A soft moan escaped her, and she dug her teeth into her bottom lip to stifle the sound. "Answer me, kitten," he purred.

"I... I understand." She should tell him to stop. She really should. She didn't.

"Good girl." Another savage smack landed across her other butt cheek. Her entire body jerked forward with the movement. She bit her lip harder. What if Abe heard them? What if someone walked by the store? The possibility of getting caught only added to her excitement and she found herself arching back towards him. His hands were gentle as they rubbed down her ass, soothing the sting before he swatted her even harder than before. Swat, rub, swat, rub. This was nothing like the play she had experienced with G. This was... so much more.

Abruptly, he stopped. He gripped her hair and roughly jerked her upright, pressing his impressive hardness against her now burning backside. He pulled her head to the side and whispered into her ear. "Just a taste, Kisa. Play with me. Let me show you how to feel."

His words touched something deep inside her. To feel. She so desperately wanted to feel. Before she could get lost in her head, he leaned down and bit her shoulder again, his teeth denting her skin through her sweater. She cried out, shoving her hips back against him. He growled, actually growled, and his teeth dug in even more roughly. Fuck. She would be bruised for sure. He released her, kissing the now sore spot. Pain and gentleness. It was a wicked mixture with Dolor.

She felt him slip something out of his pocket, then he reached around to her mouth.

"Open," he demanded. She obeyed without thought, her mind still a mixture of pleasure and pain. He slid a card between her lips and she bit down instinctively. "Such a good girl." His grip in her hair eased and he gently ran his fingers through it before stepping back. "Call me. Soon."

With that he was gone, taking his heat and leaving nothing but a cold breeze against her back.

Chapter Eleven

Kisa paced in her apartment later that week. She looked down at the card in her hand for the millionth time. They were both adults. Why couldn't they have a consensual experience together? So, they worked together, but did they really? She was on the opposite side of the building. He was a surgeon for fuck's sake. Yes, she had done some digging. Breathing out a harsh breath, Kisa pulled up a text message in her phone. She had been doing this all day, but had yet to follow through with it. Don't be a coward, Kisa, she told herself. Plugging in Dolor's number, Kisa sent him a quick text before she could chicken out.

Kisa: Hey. This is Kisa, from the hospital.

There. Easy. Did she really need to say from the hospital? She couldn't handle it if he had said Kisa who? Maybe he wouldn't even text back. It was Friday night, after all. A man like him was probably out hitting the town.

Her phone rang. She dropped it. "Shit!" Reaching down, she checked to make sure it wasn't broken. It rang again, and Dolor's number flashed on her screen. Holy fuck. She answered with shaky hands. "H... hello?"

"Took you long enough," he practically growled. Why did that turn her on so much?

"S... sorry?"

"Not yet you're not. You will be though."

Aaand there go her panties. Why did Dolor punishing her make her want to defy him more often?

"Where are you?" he asked. No small talk with him

tonight, it would seem. He sounded wound up, and Kisa felt a surge of power that she had done that to him.

"Oh, around," she said, feeling cocky as she laid back onto her couch.

"Kitten, don't fuck with me. Where?" His voice had gone deep, and pleasure shot through her core.

"I'm home." So much for her rebellion.

"Good. Get dressed. We're going out."

"O... Out? Out where?" Her heart raced as she sat up, looking around her mess of an apartment. Did she even have any clean clothes?

"Not sure yet. Wear something sexy and text me your address. Be there in an hour." With that, he hung up on her. She stared at the phone, contemplating texting him to fuck off. When did he get so bossy? Deciding having that sexy beast boss her around for an evening was better than sitting around her apartment, alone, feeling as if she was going to self-destruct at any moment, Kisa jumped up and ran to her closet. As she had expected, she had nothing to wear. Kisa never went out, and her closet consisted of PJ's, derby clothes, scrubs, sweats, and jeans. Fuck.

Sighing, Kisa headed to her laptop. Pulling up the derby private group, she debated for a solid two minutes before posting.

911. I have a date in an hour. Help.

She sat back. Looking at the post made her feel ridiculous, so she grabbed a towel and headed to the shower. She took a bit of extra care with shaving, feeling a ping of shame at the possibility of another man touching her. No sex, she promised herself. It's not like she could never be touched again. As long as her panties stayed on it would be okay.

As she stepped out of the shower, she nearly fell back in. A commotion was going on in her living room. Kisa grabbed a hairbrush for defense, clinging tightly to her towel. Peeking out the door, she felt her jaw drop. Over half the team was in her living room, spreading dresses, shoes, makeup, and even lingerie on her couch and floor.

Sly, the team captain and designated mama bear of the group, walked up and snatched the brush from her. Her warm brown eyes sparkled with kindness as she reached up and ran a hand down Kisa's soaked head. "About time," was all she said, and then the team descended.

They pulled her into the living room and made her try on outfit after outfit. They plucked and prodded and brushed, and in a blur, Kisa was dressed. They pushed her into the bathroom to look at herself. Kisa couldn't believe the reflection staring back at her. She looked gorgeous. Makeup concealed the deep shadows that normally sat beneath her eyes, the reflection of her sleepless nights. They had curled her brown hair, leaving it in soft waves down her back, and did some kind of elaborate smoky eye that she couldn't have done in a million years. She wore a dark blue dress that reminded her of Dolor's eyes. It was floor length with a plunging neckline and large slits up either side, showing off her sleek, strong legs. She looked back at the girls and felt her eyes well with tears.

"Don't even think about it!" Smack yelled, racing forward and pushing her towards a chair. "We do not have time to fix your makeup. Sit!"

Kisa sat and Smack pushed on a pair of matching heels with straps that criss-crossed up her calves. With the long slits in the dress, they would show when she walked. The entire ensemble was very Greek goddess. It made Kisa feel bold and powerful.

"You know how bad hairspray is for the ozone?" Slam complained, waving away the finishing spray Smack was pouring over Kisa's locks. They all burst out laughing, even

Kisa, much to Slam's horror. "Sure, it's all funny now. Wait until we have to breathe through cans like that movie *Spaceballs!*" This of course only made them laugh harder.

A knock sounded at the door, and all the girls froze. There was a muffled argument about them hiding, which they all refused to do, of course. Kisa rolled her eyes and headed to the door, taking a deep breath before opening it as little as possible and slipping out. She practically stumbled into Dolor in her avoidance of her overprotective clan grilling him. He gripped her shoulders, surprised, and then his eyes widened as he took her in. He pushed her back into the door, hungry eyes sliding down her dress.

"You do love testing my control, don't you, kitten," he murmured, dipping his nose to her neck. Seriously, what was with the smelling? "As much as I love the view, where is your jacket?" She closed her eyes, knowing an easy escape had been wishful thinking. Sighing, she turned and opened her door.

All of the girls had pressed themselves up against the door, attempting to eavesdrop, and looked ridiculous as they abruptly scrambled away. Dolor's eyes widened at the sight, and a grin broke out on his face.

"Ladies..."

Their faces were priceless. Shock, awe, and fear? They had taken a further step back, and Kisa looked on in confusion. She understood the awe. Look at him. Her girls had never been at a loss for words before, though. Smack seemed to recover herself the quickest, and she stepped forward with a delicate black jacket. She helped Kisa put it on, glaring daggers at Dolor. Seriously, what the hell? Dolor rubbed the back of his neck. It was both awkward and adorable.

"Take care of our girl. Or else," Smack said. Of course she did.

Kisa groaned. "Okay, thanks guys. Bye." Pushing Dolor out the door, Kisa looked back and glared at the weirdos behind her. They were sharing secretive, knowing glances, and she shook her head, deciding to ignore them for now. She would find out the scoop later.

The walk down the hallway was awkward at best. Dolor had a frown on his face, and she wanted it gone.

"So, those are your friends?" Dolor asked.

"Yes. More like family, really. They are my teammates. Roller Derby. Not the movie kind." She was rambling. Dolors' eyes had widened, and he looked impressed.

"You're part of the Vicious Valkyries?" he asked.

"You've heard of us?" Kisa was shocked. Derby was somewhat of a private community. It was everywhere, but for some reason, most people hadn't heard of it except for the old school, beat each other up kind. They still beat each other up, but with a lot more rules now.

He smiled, shaking his head. "That I have. I would love to see you skate sometime. I hear it can be quite exhilarating." His eyes slid down her body as they eased into the elevator, his hand naturally going to the small of her back. It felt possessive, and Kisa felt a small thrill at the touch.

They made idle talk about roller derby, and he truly seemed fascinated by how it was played and the rules behind it. She found conversation with him easy, and she began to relax. Then they got into his car.

If you could call it a car. It was more like a foreign animal sent from heaven. Kisa ran her hand along the sleek interior, practically purring. Adam's father had been obsessed with cars and had tried to push that love onto Adam. It didn't stick, but it had rubbed off on Kisa. She had never been in something so luxurious.

"You're a car buff," Dolor observed, staring over at her intently.

She blushed and shrugged, squirming at the intensity in his gaze. "A little. Enough to appreciate something this impressive."

Now that they were sitting in the car, she realized how tight the interior was. In such a tiny space, it was impossible to ignore the heat coming off Dolor, the smell of him soaking into her skin. He wore another fancy black suit, but the kicker was the tie. It matched his midnight blue eyes.

As her eyes were busy with her perusal, his were just as busy. She noted his gaze was plastered to her legs, and following that gaze, her blush deepened as she realized the slits showed a good portion of her thighs. She tried to straighten it, but it did little good. Squirming, Kisa looked anywhere but at him.

"It's going to be a long dinner," Dolor grumbled. He shifted in his seat and peeled out of the parking lot into the darkness beyond.

Chapter Twelve

"Seriously. This is where we're going for dinner?" Kisa stared at the building in front of her, aghast.

"Huh. Never took you for a food snob," Dolor snarked, grabbing her hand and looping it through his arm. "Suppose you wanted me to wine and dine you at some fancy five star where you leave starving?"

She shook her head, smiling back at him as they entered one of her favorite places to eat—Pizzeria Scotty. It was the best pizza in the city and Kisa felt warm all over that this is where he took her.

She had worried about going to some expensive restaurant, feeling out of place, and stressing the entire time about spending too much or spilling something. She had grown up poor. Rich people food intimidated her and kind of disgusted her at times. Escargot? More like escarg-no. Being a picky eater as an adult was damn embarrassing. Yes, she was much happier sitting down with a slice of Scotty's finest.

He led her to a round table in the back with four tall stools surrounding it and she noticed that Scotty's was kind of dead for a Friday night. The place was normally swamped. A waiter came by and took their orders. The waiter smiled way more than was natural and Kisa felt her instincts curling around in her gut. She eyed Dolor suspiciously.

"What?" he asked, faking a look of innocence.

"Why is this place so dead? And what's up with the Cheshire cat?" She nodded at smiley boy.

Dolor had the good sense to look sheepish. "I may have rented the place for the evening."

Kisa's jaw dropped. He rented the entire restaurant for a few pieces of pizza?

Dolor flashed her a dazzling grin, gripping her stool and tugging her closer. She yipped, startled, and her hand landed on his chest. He reached up, tucking her hair behind her ear. "I wanted to be able to talk freely without being interrupted or overheard. We have a few things to discuss, you and I." His hand trailed down her neck, sliding gently down her bare arm. Instant goosebumps. His mouth ticked up at the traitorous bumps. "So responsive," he murmured, his fingers continuing their dance on her arm. He didn't move away as the waiter brought out their drinks, only tipping his head in acknowledgement.

Suddenly they were very alone. She swallowed.

"So, what did you want to talk about?" she asked, taking a large drink, her mouth suddenly dry.

"Your limits, to start."

Kisa nearly spit out her mouthful at his words. She had read up on BDSM and knew about limits, but she didn't think they would just throw them out there like that. Coughing, she attempted to collect herself, her face crimson. He lifted a brow at her response.

"Um... I'm not really sure exactly. I'm a bit new at this." She twirled her straw in her drink, irritated at how unsure she sounded. He was going to think she was an amateur. She was, but he didn't have to know that. She straightened, looking him dead in the eye. "I know I have a limit with urine and fecal matter."

His eyes widened and then he threw his head back and laughed. It was such a full throated, purely happy laugh that for a moment all she could do was stare at him. He was beautiful. Then anger replaced her awe. She slapped his arm. "Don't laugh at me!"

"Oh, kitten, I'm not. You just always surprise me. No scat or watersports. Got it. What else?" His eyes still danced with humor.

"Um, none of those vacuum bag things." She squirmed thinking about them.

He nodded, looking like he was still holding back laughter, but at least he was trying to be serious.

"I guess that's it." She took another drink, feeling her blush deepen.

His eyes widened. "That's it, huh? Everything else is a green light?" She could tell he was messing with her now, and her frustration grew. He leaned in close, his words barely above a whisper, "So if I stripped you right here, tied you to this table, fucked you and then brought in that smiley waiter for a turn, you'd be just fine with that?" His words caused her pussy to clench roughly, even before the words sunk in completely. Her mouth dropped open in outrage.

"What? No, of course not!" She looked at him, horrified. He smiled broader, and she knew he was fucking with her. She scowled.

"Haven't you ever gone over terms before? You can't leave the door wide open like that, kitten. I will barge through it with a tank." He nipped at her ear playfully. Then whispered, "Besides, I don't share. Ever." She swallowed thickly.

"N... no I haven't." Beat heart. Beat. "G was the first time I had played before." She took another drink. At the silence that followed, she looked up, flinching at the look on Dolor's face. He was furious. There was a tic in his jaw, and she could practically hear his teeth grinding. It had been a long time since she had seen someone so angry.

With visible effort, his jaw released and his shoulders relaxed again.

"I'm sorry that was how your first experience went. Gideon is a joke and a mockery of the lifestyle. How did you manage to stumble upon him anyway?"

"Um...online." Kisa hated feeling scolded. It made her hackles rise, but she knew it had been pretty stupid of her.

Dolor closed his eyes, taking a deep breath and seeming to collect himself. "Okay. You're new, so I'm not gonna tan your hide. For that, anyway." He grinned. "In the future, if you want to find someone to play with, go to a munch."

Kisa's brows furrowed. "A what?"

"A munch. They are get-togethers for people in the lifestyle. They are held at restaurants and public places. People look out for each other there, and they won't let assholes take advantage of you." He took a long drink, and she tried not to stare at his throat as he swallowed. "Let's start over, okay? I am going to list some things I like to do, and you tell me if you would be willing to try them. You aren't going to know most of them, because you have never felt them before. We can do some trial and error and see what you like, okay?" His voice was calm, but tension still ran beneath it. "The biggest thing here is that you are always completely honest with me. Understood?"

Kisa nodded, his demanding tone doing funny things to her insides.

"Good girl. So, first thing is bondage. Rope, chain, collar, handcuffs... Soft limit means you are open to trying it, but wary. Hard limit means absolutely not."

Kisa swallowed again. Imagining Dolor's powerful body tying her down and having his wicked way with her. "Yes. I mean, that sounds good."

Dolor's eyes sparkled, and she could see his imagination running wild as well. "Good. Floggers, belts, and paddles?" Kisa nodded again. Would her blush ever go away? "Hot wax?" Kisa's eyes widened. She hadn't thought of that one. She nodded again, a bit more vigorously this time, and he grinned. "Nipple clamps?"

Kisa's breath stopped short. She looked down, thinking desperately. She had seen those on the websites she explored, had felt her nipples tighten in excitement, but was it too sexual? She could justify the pain play to herself. She could push back the shame and guilt eating her alive. As long as she didn't have sex, she was safe.

He gently lifted her chin, looking into her eyes. "Total honesty, kitten. It's the only way.

"Soft limit," she muttered, forcing herself not to look away. He nodded, and she saw no anger there, no disappointment.

"You control this, Kisa. Always." His words echoed with sincerity, and she nodded, feeling reassured. He ran his fingers softly down her cheek. "I know you said no sex. I need to know specifics, even if it makes you uncomfortable. My job is to push your limits without crossing them. Do you understand?"

Feeling mute, Kisa nodded again.

"Good. External play, like flogging your breasts or pussy, is that a limit?" His words were soft, as if he didn't want to startle her with them.

Her mind raced. Did those things count? They certainly weren't sex. They were pain. Right? She closed her eyes, her lips swelling. She couldn't deny the desire to experience those things with Dolor. She just wanted to be able to survive the consequences.

"Soft limit," she whispered, her voice as soft as his. He nodded, his eyes drinking in her reactions. "J... just no penetration, okay?" She stared at her hands. Had she really bitten her nails down so far?

He lifted her chin again, those midnight eyes locking onto her.

"Don't hide, kitten. You are in control here. Penetration is on the hard limit list until you tell me otherwise. Okay?" His voice made Kisa melt, and she felt her head leaning into his hand. She thought he would kiss her then. Her eyes latched onto his lips and her heart raced. Crap. She hadn't considered kissing. She had only ever kissed Adam. It somehow seemed more personal than the things they had just discussed. Dolor seemed to sense her panic and pulled back slightly.

"Okay, I think that gives us a good baseline. You always have safe words. You read about those, right? Red stops everything immediately. Yellow means you want things to slow down or you want to discuss something. That can mean everything from you needing to use the bathroom to your arm fell asleep and you need to switch positions. Green means keep going. I will ask you for your color throughout scenes, but I expect you to use your words at any time you need to. I demand it if we are to play together. I have to trust you to tell me if it's too much. Stop, don't, no... those words don't stop me. They only turn me on. Only red or yellow does. Understand?"

"Y... yes." She felt like she was going down the rabbit hole. G didn't go over any of this with her. She thought back and felt panicked. How had he expected her to tell him to stop? Would he have even listened?

"Good." Dolor stood abruptly, walking to the counter and grabbing their pizza, which had been put into a to-go box. She startled, standing as well. They weren't eating here? He held a hand out to her, and she walked to him, taking his hand as they headed to his car.

Once in the car, Kisa squirmed uncomfortably.

"Eat," Dolor demanded. Kisa looked down at the pizza box in her lap. She didn't like the order, but she was starving.

She looked at the fine upholstery. "Are you sure? This car is ridiculously nice, and I am crazy klutzy..."

He shot her a wicked grin. "I'm sure. You can't play on an empty stomach." With that sentence, she promptly dropped her pizza. Right onto her dress. He lifted a brow at her.

"Shit. I'm sorry. Did you say play? Like, tonight?" She grabbed napkins out of the glovebox and attempted to clean up her mess. Her heart was going to beat out of her chest.

"Is that a problem?" He watched her hungrily.

Was it? Hell no. She shook her head. Adrenaline started to pour through her. Was she really doing this? She hadn't been this nervous going to the club that night. What made this so different? She eyed the man beside her. He felt her gaze and looked over at her. Oh. That. That was the difference. Her panties were soaked. Again. She had a terrifying thought of her juices staining the seat beneath her and tried desperately to think of very non-sexy things. Bed sores. Gary Busey. Pickled pigs feet.

"Kitten..."

She looked over at him.

"Can I have some of that?" He nodded at the pizza.

In a daze, she lifted a piece of pizza from the box, holding it to his mouth. Transfixed, she watched as he took a huge bite. She thought of his teeth sinking into her shoulder. Fuck, the upholstery was doomed.

"Where are we going?" Kisa asked, her voice all too husky. How could feeding a piece of pizza to someone be so sexy?

"To the club."

Kisa bristled at his words. She had hoped for somewhere a bit more private this time around.

"I have a private suite there. I help run the place."

Kisa was stunned. Of course he did. A surgeon by day, sex club partner by night.

In what seemed like minutes, Dolor pulled up behind the club. He slid into a VIP parking spot in the employee parking area, got out, and came to her side to help her out of the car. They left the pizza and headed towards the back entrance. A large man with green hair guarded the door. He was huge, looking down even at Dolor's six plus feet. He smiled warmly and stepped to the side.

"Boss." His voice was the deepest Kisa had ever heard. Dolor nodded at him as they went by. Those dark green eyes shimmered and he winked at Kisa, causing her to blush yet again.

She expected to have to go through the club, but this seemed to be an entirely different wing. Dolor gripped her hand tightly as they entered and led her to the left and down a dark stairway. She swallowed, her nerves kicking up another notch. There was an old-fashioned vibe the deeper they went and electric lights were soon replaced with wall torches.

"This isn't an elaborate ruse so that you can sacrifice me or something, is it?"

Dolor's teeth flashed in the dim lighting, and he squeezed her hand in reassurance. "Mattheus has a penchant for old things. It makes his tastes a bit unique."

"That's not a no," Kisa grumbled, making Dolor laugh. They came to another level, and a hall branched off to the side. "I can't believe all of this is under here. The architecture is amazing."

"It is. It was a main source for smuggling alcohol back

in the day." He looked amused at that, and she wondered what the joke was.

They got to a wooden door at the end of the hall and he pulled a key from his pocket. The key, like everything else down the hall, looked ancient. Dolor unlocked and opened the door, leading Kisa inside and shutting the door behind her. She jumped at the sound of the lock clicking.

The room was huge and immaculate, with a massive four-poster bed on the far side. The bed was draped in black bedding, blood red pillows propped neatly by the headboard. Elegant décor was scattered across the room, and Kisa wanted to soak it all in. Some of the things on the shelves looked like antiques. Curiosity burned within her, and Kisa was startled to feel it. When was the last time she had felt curious about anything?

Heat against her back indicated that Dolor had closed the distance. Her pulse thundered in her veins and she tugged at her dress. Dolor's voice was low when he finally spoke.

"Are you sure about this, Kisa? You can stop it at any time." He brushed her hair to the side, running his fingers down her neck and across her collarbone. She shivered and nodded. "I need to hear you say it, kitten."

"I'm sure." And she was. She needed this. She wanted this.

"What are your safe words?" he murmured, his fingers dragging her zipper down slowly.

Her words felt thick as she spoke them. "Green, yellow, red." He was gentle as he slid the silk from her shoulders, stepping away from her as the fabric fell to her feet. She felt his gaze on her backside and silently thanked Smack for the lingerie. It was a dark blue, and she knew it looked good with the paleness of her skin. The panties weren't quite a thong but revealing enough that most of her ass was on display for him.

His hands were tender on her shoulders, caressing her as if she were glass. "Color, kitten?"

She blew out a breath. Now or never. "Green, sir." He groaned at the addition, and she smirked. Then he was pushing her shoulders down, shoving her to her knees. She kneeled there on the dark gray carpet, awkwardly at first, keeping her eyes down as she heard him walk around to her front. Her breasts rose and fell with her breaths.

"Fucking perfect. You were born for this. This is how I want you when we play, on your knees before me. Spread your legs and sit back on your heels. Palms up on your thighs." She did so, the cool air caressing her damp panties and making her shiver.

He walked away, and she couldn't help but watch him, seeing him undo his tie and the top button of his dress shirt. He slid his suit jacket off his broad shoulders, laying it on a chair beside a small table. He headed to the closet, opening the doors and stepping inside. It must have been huge. Kisa squirmed, wondering if she was supposed to be doing something.

Then he was walking back towards her. Her eyes devoured him. He was stunning, and the archaic lighting only accentuated that beauty. He held a large, crimson rope in his hand, and she was pulled back into the moment.

"Give me your arms."

She reached out, and he turned her palms down, pushing her wrists together. She expected him to simply tie them together, but what he did was almost art. He looped the rope in an elaborate tie, twisting and turning it all the way up her forearms, leaving about three feet of length loose. She tried to move her wrists apart but found little wiggle room. He nodded, satisfied, and jerked the remaining length of rope, dragging her to her feet.

"Color."

"Green, sir."

Nodding again, he led her so she faced the end of the elaborate bed. Then he roughly pushed her forward. She fell awkwardly onto her stomach, her arms unable to stop her fall. He chuckled, leaning over and grabbing the length of rope once more. He drew her arms so she was reaching above her head and tied her to the headboard. Her face was turned to the side, and she listened as he moved away from the bed. Where was he going?

She heard a clatter and jerked against the rope. Her heart raced, and she listened desperately for a clue as to what he was doing. She jumped again when something soft trailed up her feet, over her shaking thighs, across her backside, and continued up her back. Goosebumps followed in its wake, and she tried turning to see what tool he had.

"Stay still," he ordered.

She attempted to stop her squirming.

Suddenly, the softness was gone. She cried out as it came down against her ass. It wasn't hard exactly, not nearly as hard as G had done it, but she felt like her nerves were on fire. Every sensation, every sound seemed heightened to her.

"This is a flogger. There are many different kinds, but this is my favorite." He began a pattern, bringing the flogger down again and again against her back, ass, and thighs.

It felt like an intense massage, and she felt her body flushing with pleasure. There wasn't any pain, and she wondered again at the direction of this play.

As if reading her mind, Dolor said, "This is called a

warm up, I am getting your body adjusted to the different sensations. Awakening your nerves so that when we do decide to play harder, we can get you to where you need to go without resorting to brute force. There is a skill to playing, and preparing your body is part of it."

His hands ran down the length of her body and she closed her eyes at the sensation. Her skin felt like it was on fire.

"Now you're ready," he murmured, before bringing his hand down roughly against her ass. She cried out, the sensation more intense than when he had done it in the bookstore. Her breathing was loud in the room as he ran his palm over the sting before bringing it down hard on the other cheek. She cried out again and shifted on the bed.

"Hold still," he growled, smacking her again, this time on her thigh.

He did the same pattern as he had at the bookstore, bouncing back and forth between smacking and rubbing the sting out. Kisa felt the pain radiating down her legs and causing an ache within her core. Her pussy felt swollen, and she knew she had soaked through her panties by now. She was beyond caring as he increased the strength of his swats. His last slap had her jerking from the bed, coming up to her knees. He gripped her thighs, leaning forward and running his lips across her burning flesh. She wiggled under his tender kisses.

"Color, kitten." His voice was nothing but gravel and lust.

"G... green, sir," she stuttered and gasped. Her entire body was shaking, and she realized that by pulling her knees up she had pushed her ass closer to his face. He groaned as he rubbed a gentle hand up her thigh, feeling the wetness there.

"Such a good girl," he whispered, leaning forward and biting her ass.

"Fuck!" she cried out, jerking at the sharp bite. What was with him and biting?

He chuckled, standing back up at the end of the bed. He had left enough slack on the rope to be able to move her around as needed and he used that now as he grabbed her ankles and jerked her back towards him roughly. He set her feet on the floor, leaning over her waist. She wiggled at feeling him press into her tender backside, gasping as his cock pressed into her ass. He was huge, and she thanked the derby gods they weren't having sex. He ran kisses between her shoulder blades and down her spine. She felt her body relax again until the heat of his body left her once more.

She shivered in the cool breeze. Suddenly, a loud smack echoed in the room followed by a solid pain across her ass. Kisa's back arched, her gasp sounding more like a moan than she was comfortable with. Dolor, of course, noticed.

He chuckled, smoothing the ache with his hand. "Like that one, did you? That's called a paddle. The noise makes it sound rougher than it is."

Smack! Her thighs began to shake. Kisa leaned up on her toes, arching towards the paddle.

"Greedy woman..." Dolor's approving voice, mixed with the sound and sting of the paddle, had Kisa shivering all over. She felt like her body was coming apart, as if at any moment she might explode and fly away. It was intense, and Kisa didn't know whether to be afraid or run into the feeling head on.

Is this what Smack had meant? The high she was supposed to be chasing? The paddle stopped and Dolor once again leaned his body over hers, rubbing those gentle hands down her welts. Her eyes closed and she sighed, loving the feel of it.

"Color," Dolor whispered, his command sounding like an endearment.

"Green. So much green."

Dolor kissed her cheek reverently, and she basked in it.

"One more toy tonight, I think." She didn't want this to end, but she trusted him. She knew that he understood more about this than she did. That he knew how much she could handle.

The whistling should have been her first warning. Something that made that type of noise couldn't be any good. Something whipped through the air, the light sound barely audible, followed by an intense sting across her thighs. She cried out in pain, jerking against the bed roughly. The way he had pulled her to the edge of the bed caused her body to push against the mattress when she jerked, her swollen clit throbbing at the contact. His hand didn't soothe as much this time as he ran it over her heated flesh. She tried to wriggle away from him, but his firm hands held her in place. The pain of his touch mixed with the pressure on her clit.

"Color." His voice shook as he stood over her, watching her writhe.

She paused this time, debating if she could handle more. Her feelings swirled within her. She wasn't sure where pain left off and pleasure began. "G..g..green, sir..." she gasped out, her voice raw.

"You're doing so well, kitten," he purred. "Your ass is so pretty and red. This is a cane, Kisa, and I don't use it lightly. Two more. Can you handle two more?"

Two more. She could do it. She would do it.

"Yes, sir." She steeled herself, her entire body tensing.

"You have to relax, darling. Relax." He rubbed his

hands down her back, soothing her. Kisses followed his hands and she slowly felt her body ease. *Swack!*

"Fuck!" she screamed. She jerked against the rope again, feeling tears sting her eyes. She hated the cane. Despised it. Her juices ran down her thighs, trying to make a liar out of her, and she felt his fingers trace up their trail, gathering her wetness.

He leaned over her, looking into her eyes.

"Open," he growled, staring at her mouth. She obeyed, and he slid his finger between her lips. She whimpered as she tasted his skin mixed with her arousal. His eyes grew darker, and he growled as he watched her. He drew away, leaving her panting.

Swack! The last strike had her nearly sobbing as she collapsed onto the bed. With that last, brutal stroke, Kisa's first mental shield shattered.

Chapter Thirteen

Forty-three... forty-four... forty-five... Kisa gasped, her small feet pushing herself from the bottom of the motel pool, the wind cool against her skin as she swallowed lungfuls of air. Her eyes were blurry, the old chlorine making her nostrils burn as she steadied her heartbeat. She glanced towards their end of the motel, the copper curtains pulled back enough to see her parents in the small space. Their faces were contorted in rage, and Kisa looked away, biting her lip. Their words reached her all the same.

It was payday, and that was always a rough day, or night, or week. She knew ahead of time to be ready to go elsewhere, darting out the door the moment her dad's beat up pick-up idled in the parking lot. Her mother greeted him at the door, one hand on her plump hip, the other outstretched for the check she already knew was gone. His defeated gaze and bloodshot eyes were enough, and the vicious cycle began again.

At ten years old, Kisa knew all about her father's addictions and the battles waged among her family over them. Sometimes she would be at school and wonder at how the other children didn't seem to have those same worries. He was a good daddy, and she loved him despite the war that raged in him. As tears began to well, Kisa breathed deeply, diving back into the water, the crushing weight drowning out the bitter words being spewed. Longer... She could hold her breath a little longer...

Dolor gasped, coming out of the memory. Anger thundered through him towards Kisa's father, mixing with pride in her strength. She had been through so much. No wonder she had built such fierce shields.

Time had held still, and he looked down at the shaking form before him. He hadn't drunk too much. She was still awake. He let out a relieved breath. He knew his eyes were black as night and he closed them, trying to calm himself so he could finish. She needed him now. The feeding had been unlike anything he had ever felt. Her walls had fallen and before he knew it, he was sucked within them. It was as if she had pulled him into her. He sometimes got memories from those he fed on, but it was rare. Hers had been sharp like he had been placed into a movie. He had been her, felt her emotions, felt her pain, and he had feasted.

He reached out with his darkness, sliding the shadows against her mind. Her walls were back up, but there was a crack now. He jerked his shadows back, afraid of being sucked in once more. He had fed too deeply if what he was feeling was any indication. Any more and he would risk harming her. With shaking hands, Dolor reached for Kisa's wrists, gently untying her from the headboard and removing the rope.

Kisa was... smiling. He shook his head, reveling in the peaceful look on her face. It was a rare sight and it gave her a gentle beauty. Rubbing her wrists where the ropes had bit into her skin, Dolor crawled onto the bed. He rested against the headboard and pulled her onto his lap. She didn't protest. She was flying high, soaring through subspace. It was the perfect point where adrenaline and endorphins combined, the chemicals causing a euphoric high. It was one of the things that made playing hard so dangerous. If a sadist wasn't careful with a true masochist, he could break them. They would just keep asking for more. This was a place without pain and Dolor was grateful he had been there to prevent Gideon from having his way with her. He wouldn't have stopped. He would have broken this beautiful creature and left her for the wolves.

Dolor slid his fingers through Kisa's hair and she sighed, content. He had never felt the urge to play with hair before, but something about hers intrigued him. Her chocolate waves were soft and if one looked closely, you could see the barest hint of red here and there. Dolor smiled. Kisa's breathing had evened out and he wondered if she had fallen asleep.

"Thank you," she whispered, snuggling closer to him.

He looked down at her in awe. He was getting too attached and he knew it. He couldn't keep her. This ache in his chest, this need for her, was supposed to have lessened after he had gotten a taste of her. Instead, he craved her even more desperately. He kissed the top of her head and lowered her gently to the bed. He grabbed a sheet from the closet and covered her carefully. Her eyes were still closed and that smile hadn't left yet.

He headed towards his bathroom at the back of the suite. Once there, Dolor splashed water on his face and stared at his reflection. Damn it. His shadows had filled his eyes, the stars within them startling. Dolor breathed deeply. They normally only did that when he fed completely, sucking the life force away entirely from a being. He hadn't done that in a very long time. Sometimes they would flicker with intense emotions but never stick like this.

Wincing, he reached down and adjusted his cock. It had been hard since he had first seen her come out of that apartment. The apartment with those women... Shaking his head, Dolor decided to address that problem another day.

Dolor hopped in the shower. He reached down and gripped his firm cock, thinking about the delicious woman passed out on his bed. She would be asleep for a while, and he needed to gain some control. Easing himself could only help. Remembering her tight body squirming before him, her ass arching back, the wetness that had trailed down her legs... His bedroom would smell like her lust for weeks. He saw stars as he came, his body jerking as he imagined painting her red backside with his seed.

"Fuck..." he groaned, resting his forehead on the cool tile for several minutes. Shaking his head, Dolor got out of the shower and wrapped a towel around his waist.

He turned and set up a bath, making sure the water was a bit cooler than normal. Her skin would be sensitive and anything too hot would sting. He grabbed some frilly bubbly stuff out from underneath the sink that Mattheus had given him for Christmas years ago. At least the joke would get some use. Squirting it in the bath, Dolor straightened and looked back at the mirror. His eyes had returned to normal. Thank God. Taking a deep breath, Dolor turned off the bath and left the bathroom, prepared to scoop up his kitten and give her the care she would need after such a scene.

Problem was, his kitten was gone. The bed lay empty, the dress and shoes nowhere in sight.

Chapter Fourteen

Kisa's feet were freezing as she made her way back up the staircase, but there was no way she was navigating these steps again in heels, especially with how wobbly she felt. She wasn't sure how long she and Dolor had been occupied, but she hoped the club would be dead enough so that no one saw her walk of shame. Well, walk of oh-my-did-that-seriously-just-happen. She didn't really feel shame. Not yet, anyway. She felt... great. Perfect really. Her brain was pleasantly cloudy. Her body felt relaxed, and she still had that stupid smile on her face.

So what if Dolor had left her laying there. What did she think he was going to do? This wasn't a relationship. This was an exchange, nothing more. She pushed back at the ache caused by that thought. She didn't want, couldn't have, a relationship. Her soul was Adam's and always would be. Better for her to leave now without any awkward conversation.

Kisa silently thanked her dad for her sense of direction as she stumbled up the steps. He had been a truck driver and for whatever reason, his weird skill of always being able to remember directions had rubbed off on her.

Suddenly, Kisa was staring at a very large, very bare chest. She followed that tree trunk chest up into one of the sexiest faces she had ever seen. Not as sexy as Dolor's of course, but damn. What did they put in the water here? He had smooth, mocha colored skin, full smirking lips, and green eyes that sparkled with mischief. He wore a fedora, which seemed a bit odd with his shirtless state.

"Hello, little one. What are you doing down here?" His

voice was deep and taunting, promising dark things. She swallowed thickly.

"I... I was just leaving..." She moved to walk past him, and he shot an arm out, bracing it against the wall in front of her.

"What's the rush? You came down here for a reason, no?" He had an accent she couldn't place, and she backed up a step. Did he think she was down here snooping?

"Dolor brought me. And I really do have to get going now." She ducked under his arm and started back up the steps. His eyes had widened at her pronouncement, a look of shock crossing his face. Did she really look so unworthy? She reached up and smoothed her hair. It was a mess. She had been in such a state when she left that she didn't even consider her appearance. Lord, she must have makeup all over her face.

The man was in front of her again. His smile made her blink stupidly. He really was too pretty.

"My apologies little one. I didn't realize Dolor had brought a guest over." He bowed low, his hat barely managing to stay on his head. He somehow made the old world gesture look natural. "I am Mattheus. I run this lovely establishment with Dolor. Apparently, I need to discuss manners with my friend. Leaving a pretty thing like you to walk out by your lonesome. Please." He offered her his muscular arm, and she carefully slid her own arm into it. Her legs were still jelly, after all.

They continued slowly up the staircase. She found Mattheus quite charming. What should have been a quick trip, seemed to take forever as Kisa tried to focus on her feet instead of the pleasant fog coating her normally chaotic mind.

Mattheus didn't seem to mind her pace and filled the time by riddling her with questions. He asked about what she did for work and seemed fascinated by radiology, which was weird. No one was fascinated by that. He was easy to talk to though, and she realized her good mood and hazy brain had her more open than usual.

They reached the back entrance, and Kisa groaned as she remembered she hadn't brought her phone. Well, shit. At her pause, Mattheus looked her over. Noticing she didn't have a purse, he asked her where her keys were.

"Um, Dolor drove." She fidgeted nervously.

He turned and scowled down the stairs, almost as if he could see Dolor down there.

"Could I use your phone to call a cab?" Why the hell hadn't she brought a clutch and her phone? She was so used to wearing scrubs with a million pockets, and so not used to the limitations of fancy dresses.

Mattheus waved a large hand at her.

"Nonsense. Charles will give you a ride anywhere you need to go." He nodded at Charles who still stood outside the door. Kisa blinked at the goliath, wondering if his skin held a green tint in the moonlight or if it was just her imagination. "I am going to go have words with my good friend." His tone implied the words would not be friendly.

"Oh, please don't. Really, it's no big deal. I don't want to inconvenience anyone." She shook her head, ready to escape and enjoy her buzz alone.

"Not a debate, sweet-thing." With that, he pushed her gently towards Charles who gave her a kind smile, offering his arm.

Why were the men here so bossy and strangely gentlemanly? Knowing it was pointless to argue, Kisa took the arm that was about the size of her torso and headed towards the parking lot. She turned around to say thanks to Mattheus, but he was already gone.

Dolor was halfway up the stairs before he ran into Mattheus. His heart was racing and he tried to calm himself. He had run out of the suite with the towel still wrapped around his waist. He wanted to catch Kisa before she left and knew she couldn't have gotten far. He had driven, for fuck's sake. Mattheus' knowing smirk told him it was too late.

"Pretty little thing, she is. Decide you wanted seconds?" Mattheus smirked, seeing his undressed state. "Perhaps when you're finished I could have a go?"

The words had barely left his mouth before Dolor moved, his face inches from Mattheus.

Mattheus narrowed his eyes, his posture still lazy. "Thought so. She's what's got you so distracted as of late, is she not?"

Dolor turned, his hand running through his damp hair. "I'm handling it," he said, walking back towards his suite.

"Obviously," Mattheus said in a flat tone, clearly unconvinced. "I need you on top of your game right now, brother. We can't afford any distractions, not with the Helic contract looming over our heads. We are only going to have one shot at this. You need to leave the girl be." His tone was serious, a rarity for him.

"I know. I'll deal with it." Dolor gritted his teeth, knowing he had been trying and failing to do just that. He paused before going through his door. He hated to ask, afraid it would show just how fucked he was.

Before the words could force themselves out, Mattheus slapped his back in understanding.

"I sent her with Charles. He'll get her home." Turning to leave, Mattheus shook his head, clearly dumbfounded by the turn of events.

Dolor called after him, "Thank you, brother."

Mattheus simply waved a farewell and headed to his suite.

Dolor went through his door, wincing at the smell of the lust still lingering there. Mattheus was right. Kisa was a distraction. One he didn't need right now, not when they were so close to fulfilling everything they had worked for. Sighing, Dolor headed to his closet, swearing to let her go.

He lasted six hours. Six hours before he slammed the door in frustration and left for Kisa's apartment. Just a few more feeds. Just a little more and he would be cured of this madness.

Chapter Fifteen

Kisa was not feeling so hot. The ride back to her place had been quiet. Charles wasn't much for small talk. She squirmed in the plush backseat, her backside still burning from where Dolor had swatted her. She shuddered just thinking about it. It was one of the most intimate, intense experiences of her life. She wondered if that was the only time she would feel such a thing, and quickly decided against it. Oh, she was definitely doing that again. If Dolor didn't want her, surely there would be someone else. She could go to one of those munch things he mentioned. She frowned, a chill sweeping through her. She didn't like the idea of experiencing that with anyone else. She wanted Dolor.

As they got to her apartment, Kisa turned to say a quick goodbye to Charles before opening her door. Squeaking, Kisa shrunk back against the door before she could open it.

"Something the matter, Miss?" Charles' deep voice asked, but Kisa couldn't answer. She could only stare at the massive, green giant in the front seat. The shape was generally the same, but Charles skin was definitely green.

Collecting herself, Kisa frantically reached for the car's elusive doorknob.

"I'm fine. Just fine. Um, thanks for the ride!" Her voice was high and terrified as she practically fell out of the car. Charles only frowned, no doubt wondering where Dolor had picked up the crazy one this time. She felt him watching her as she went into her apartment complex, but she didn't look back.

Her hands were shaking so hard that it took her three tries to get her door unlocked. What the hell was wrong with her? That was the second time now that someone had turned green before her eyes. Maybe she had a cataract? She had heard of x-ray techs getting those if they weren't careful with their exposure to radiation. That must be it. She would set up an appointment with the eye doctor next week. Deflect, deflect, deflect. Kisa knew something was seriously wrong with her, but she could feel her brain trying to make up excuses to reason away her crazy. She happily allowed it.

The rest of the night went by smoothly. Kisa's buzz remained throughout the morning and she found herself dancing around the kitchen as she cleaned, blaring the music on the radio. She never listened to music anymore and she certainly never cleaned. She felt reborn.

And then, as if someone poked a hole in her happy balloon, Kisa deflated. She looked around at her spotless, empty apartment, and burst into tears. She didn't really know why she was crying. It wasn't the usual slow crying she did over Adam, or the mournful crying she sometimes had over her parents. This was gut-wrenching, irrational sobbing. She cried as she grabbed a towel, cried harder as she undressed and felt the pain across her backside, and practically fell apart when she caught a glimpse of her ass in the mirror.

There was an array of colors on her bottom. Three large welts striped across her thighs in a neat row, from that blasted cane no doubt. Splotches of red and purple covered her ass, and she could see where her blood vessels had blown in certain sections. She gingerly touched a particularly deep violet spot, wincing. Her eyes slid up her back, noting the lack of marks. He had focused mostly on her ass and thighs. She reached her face and her sobbing abruptly faltered. Her eyes were... alive. They glowed, with misery, yes, but they had life there. They weren't dead. She wasn't dead.

A hard knock sounded at the door and Kisa jumped. Grabbing her robe off the door, she quickly used the towel she had grabbed to dry her face. Her eyes were swollen and she knew she looked dreadful from crying so hard. She opened the door slightly, gasping as it was forcefully pushed open the rest of the way. Six feet of pissed off man stormed into her apartment.

"You left," he growled, eyes searching the apartment.

Well, thank goodness she had cleaned.

She closed the door and turned to face him. Dolor whirled on her, his anger dimming as his eyes roved over her face.

"Oh, kitten." He moved to her and to her utter embarrassment, she burst into tears. Again. Without a word, he gathered her into his arms, lifting her gently. She instinctively wrapped her legs around his waist. She gasped as she remembered a little too late that she was naked under her robe, her core pressed against him. Good gravy, was this man always hard?

She shuddered in his arms, burying her face into his neck and taking in his scent. He shushed her as he held her gently to him.

"Bedroom," he demanded, and she pointed without lifting her face. He walked with her easily and his strength comforted her somehow. When they got to the bedroom, he set her gingerly on the bed. He seemed to sniff suddenly and his jaw tightened again. Looking around the bedroom, he seemed to be searching for something.

"Do you live with someone?" he said, his fists clenched.

"N...no. Why?" Her voice sounded like sandpaper.

He shook his head, seeming to clear it. "Why did you

leave?" His words were gentle, but she could hear the hardness beneath them. He was upset. With her?

"I...I just assumed we were finished." She looked down at her bare feet. When she looked back up, he was staring down at her with exasperation, his hands buried in his hair.

"Kitten. I don't know if I'll ever be finished with you. Now lay that naughty ass down. On your belly." His words made her heart race, even as the thought of another scene so soon made her wince.

"Dolor...I don't think I can. I'm pretty sore..." She hated to say no to him, but there was just no way that was happening.

His eyes softened and he reached forward, running his hand down her hair.

"Trust me. Lie down." Strangely, she did trust him. She lay down, nervous all the same. She heard him rustling in his pockets and her heart picked up speed. "Before you decided to go and make assumptions, I was drawing you a bath. I'm assuming from your responses that with all your research on this lifestyle, you never actually researched the after portion."

She blushed. She really hadn't. What did she care about what happened after?

"Aftercare is what we do after a scene. It's important and can make the drop easier, not to mention save you from damage to your skin or an infection." His words were soft as he raised her robe over her hips, baring her to the waist.

She heard the sharp intake of his breath as he gazed at her nakedness and she squirmed as a gentle finger traced a painful welt.

"Does it make me a monster that seeing my marks on you turns me on?" he murmured, almost to himself. She had had the same response looking at them in the mirror. Dangerous ground.

"What's a drop?" she deflected, having to clear her throat before the words would come out. As if snapping him out of a daze, Dolor moved back away from her, setting some things down on her dresser. She couldn't see them from her position on the bed and her curiosity perked up again.

"You know that when someone gets high off of something they have to come down. Drugs, caffeine, endorphins. It all works the same. You burned up all of your endorphins and now your body is realizing it. It can make for a rough day." He had walked back towards her, crouching beside the bed and looking into her eyes. He traced a finger down her cheek. "You shouldn't drop alone. I wish you would have stayed." He looked so sad.

She turned her cheek, gently kissing the finger that had trailed her face. Her eyes widened when she realized what she had done. It was so natural with him. Embarrassed, she buried her face into the mattress. His hand stroked her hair, and then he was sliding those hands down her body.

"We didn't break any skin. You won't need any antiseptic cream." He was methodical as he checked her wounds.

She clenched her thighs together. Being near him always shot straight to her sex. It was frustrating and exhilarating. He was a complete professional as he evaluated her and Kisa's mind started to wander down porno territory. Doctor porn suddenly didn't seem so absurd. His words pulled her out of the fantasy abruptly.

"I would like to give you a bath. Would you let me?"

She shuddered. Would she? She hadn't been completely naked with anyone since... Tears welled again. What was she doing? This was the same apartment she had shared with Adam. How could she be acting like this here?

"Kitten?" His voice was close and she opened her tightly shut eyes. He was kneeling by the bed once more, searching her face. "No sex. I just want to make sure your muscles don't knot up. Okay?"

She swallowed and nodded. His voice was so sweet and understanding. Why was he being so kind to her?

He smiled. "I'm going to run the bath. Do not leave this time, understand?"

She let out a choked giggle. "I... I'll be here."

"Good." He kissed her nose and stood. Taking off his suit jacket, he tossed it onto the rocking chair in the corner, rolling up his sleeves over muscled forearms as he sought out her bathroom. Dolor was here. He was taking care of her. Her entire life she had taken care of everyone around her. Adam had been the lone exception and when he died, she thought she would never feel cared for again.

Dolor came back moments later, reaching down and scooping her off the bed. She wrapped her legs around him again. It was really the only way to keep her sore ass from being pressed against him. Yeah, that was why she did it. His hands remained at her waist, keeping away from her bruises. He set her on her feet in the bathroom, and her nerves kicked in. He looked into her eyes as he reached for the tie on her robe. Her body wouldn't stop shaking, but she held his gaze as the robe fell. He was a doctor. He saw it all the time. They were adults. What's a little bit of nudity among friends? She told herself all of these things even as a deep blush flushed across her chest.

He kept his eyes on hers as he turned her, urging her to step into the clawfoot tub. It was full of bubbles, and it made her feel like a little kid again. She never took bubble baths.

"It's cold," Kisa complained, her arms going over her chest. The chill had instantly gone to her nipples, causing them to harden. Stupid physics. Dolor gently urged her into the cool water.

"It's necessary. A hot bath would have hurt." His voice held no heat, and she was surprised to feel a bit put off that her naked wetness wasn't affecting him at all.

She glanced back at him and felt her heart stop. His eyes held all of the heat his voice didn't. She watched his throat bob as he swallowed.

"Eyes forward, kitten." There it was. That hint of a growl.

She obeyed, looking ahead at the pale blue tile and pulling her knees up tightly to her chest. Her body started to relax in the water, the tension in her muscles easing. Her head lolled forward, resting against her knees as she held herself together. He grabbed her lime green loofa off the edge of the tub, getting it wet and running it down her shoulders. He washed her back gently and seemed to be taking his time.

When he stopped, she lifted her head from her knees, dropping back in the tub and facing the ceiling. Her eyes closed and she sighed in contentment as her soul finally seemed to calm. Kisa opened her eyes at the silence, wondering where Dolor had gone. He was still kneeling behind her, his hungry gaze following the lean line of her neck towards her chest. When she had leaned her head back, the tops of her breasts had escaped their bubble shield.

She held her breath as she watched him. She was fascinated by his reactions to her body and she felt herself grow wet as he devoured her with his eyes. She didn't move to cover herself as she normally would have and his eyes moved to hers. She knew he saw the hunger reflected back at him, but she couldn't make herself care. Her body and emotions had been too much for her to handle today, and she didn't have the energy to mask them now.

Slowly he reached forward, grabbing the loofa out of the water. His fingers slid against her thigh in the process and she closed her eyes again. God, how she wanted to be touched. She hadn't allowed herself to come since Adam, not even by her own hand. She couldn't. She had tried a few times, but the loneliness consumed her before she could accomplish it. She gasped as cool water suddenly soaked her neck, the water sliding down to her breasts. Her eyes snapped open and she saw that more bubbles had washed away with the water.

Dolor looked at her wickedly, reaching down to soak the loofa again. She watched as he raised it above her chest.

"Color," he whispered, holding the loofa above her. She swallowed thickly.

"Green." She said it so quietly, she wondered if he had heard her. He nodded and squeezed the loofa. The water poured across her breasts, and she looked down at them as they were revealed. Her nipples were painfully hard from the cold and the lust coursing through her. Her breathing was coming quicker, and with every rise of her chest, her nipples threatened to breach the water.

"So fucking perfect." Her eyes snapped to his at the reverence in his words. He stared at her breasts with obvious admiration. Pride swelled in her chest. She did have good boobs. He licked his bottom lip and she imagined him leaning forward, taking one hard tip between his teeth. She bit her lip to stop the moan sitting in her throat.

Dolor closed his eyes, looking almost pained. "Alright, I think you've soaked long enough." He stood and walked into the hall, searching her cabinets for the towels. Finding one, he walked back, holding it open for her.

She suddenly felt unsure. He hadn't really looked at her when she got into the bath. Something had passed between them though. She felt like they had crossed a line and she wasn't sure if they could go back. Rising, she decided to keep her back to him, hiding the last intimate part of her he hadn't seen.

"Arms up." That gravel voice of his was not helping matters any. She raised shaking arms and nearly whimpered as he wrapped the towel tightly around her, his fingers brushing the tops of her breasts. How was it that this man made innocent touches seem so much more intense? He could do more to her body with soft touches than she could ever accomplish directly with her own hands.

He lifted her out of the tub, setting her on her feet. "Back into the bedroom," he ordered. He seemed to have recaptured some of his lost control. She felt that stab of disappointment again. He must have read it on her face because he gripped her hair roughly, jerking her head back and leaning over her. "Make no mistake, kitten. My control is hanging by a thread. There is nothing more I want right now than to devour every inch of you. However, seeing how that is off the table, I am going to do the next best thing. I'm going to take care of you. Got it?"

Her own self-control teetered. Why wasn't she letting him take her? Why did she keep resisting? He must have seen that too, because he groaned and released her hair, gently pushing her towards the bedroom.

Once there, he sat down on the edge of the bed, pulling her between his thighs. She watched as he slowly undid her towel, wanting to reach down and shield her core from him. She squirmed and he stopped, looking up at her before letting the towel drop.

"Color?"

"G... green." He wasn't throwing her down and fucking her. He said he was going to take care of her. She could handle this. He smiled, and the smile was that of a man before a feast. Oh, fuck. Maybe she couldn't handle this. Before she could think more about protesting, he dropped the towel.

Instinctively, she reached forward to hide herself, but he gripped her hands and pulled them behind her back. He altered his grip so that he held both of her wrists in his one massive hand. Then he leaned back. She could do nothing but stand there as his eyes slid down every inch of her. She blushed when his gaze dipped lower, his mouth parting slightly. She was bare. She didn't do it for any sexual reason, obviously. It was simply more comfortable, especially with the leggings she wore for derby.

He leaned forward and her breathing stopped. Was he going to kiss her there? Was she ready for that? Instead, his lips slid across her abdomen, his tongue sliding across her belly button, his teeth grazing the flesh on her side. He released her wrists and leaned back, his breathing harsh. She saw his erection pressing against his pants and her eyes widened. Even if she did decide to take that step with him eventually, he would never fit. It was impossible. The cocky grin he flashed her told her that he saw where her gaze had landed and that he would make it fit. She swallowed.

"Enough tempting my self-control today, kitten. Lay on the bed on your belly again." His voice was playful and she smirked back, liking that side of him.

Oh, who was she kidding, she liked every side of him.

He slid off the bed and she lay down on her belly as instructed. A few moments later, something cold squirted across her ass. She jerked up, her head whipping around. He was smiling, his eyes laughing at her as he held up a bottle of lotion. She blushed furiously and buried her face back into the mattress. If only he knew just how wet it made her to think about him coming on her ass like that. Then he would have really been laughing.

He groaned, and she looked behind her again. He was staring down, his eyes roving over the mess of white lotion he had made. His eyes locked with hers, and she knew at that moment they were on the same mental wavelength. He growled and shook his head, reaching forward and gently rubbing the lotion into her roughened skin. She winced and squirmed. It hadn't seemed to hurt this much the night before.

"Tomorrow the pain will be worse. It's always roughest the second day." His words were now doctorly.

She breathed a sigh of relief. She could handle Dr. Dolor much more easily than the walking panty destroying version.

"That's like derby. We're always the sorest two days after a bout," she mused. He grunted in response, focused on his task. "Why didn't I drop after the club?"

Dolor snorted. "It takes more than a brute with a tool to get someone to subspace. If you aren't there mentally, you can't let go enough to space out. Did you feel the same high after playing with Gideon?"

It was Kisa's turn to snort. "Definitely not."

"There you have it."

After the lotion had been rubbed in thoroughly, probably a bit too thoroughly really, Dolor kissed one of her tender cheeks and then the other. There was something endearing about his tenderness.

"Get dressed and meet me in the kitchen." He left her

room without another word, and she felt the chill creep back in.

She hurriedly got up, looking through her drawers for something non-hideous to wear. She grabbed her go-to leggings but winced at the thought of the tight material hugging her heated bottom. She grabbed a pair of blue flannel pjs instead and a black tank top with a built in bra. It made her boobs look good. Not that she cared what her boobs looked like or anything.

She grabbed her brush on the way to the kitchen. She saw him standing at her fridge looking at her abysmal selection. He must have heard her enter because without looking, he pointed back at one of her stools and commanded, "Sit."

She rolled her eyes, but when she saw he had laid one of the couch throw pillows down on the hard stool, her heart softened. She sat, and he put a large glass of water in front of her along with two ibuprofen.

"It will help with the pain," he said gently, grabbing the brush from her hand.

She couldn't move as he began to work the brush through her hair. It was such a simple gesture, and so profound. She couldn't remember the last time her mother had brushed her hair. It made her feel incredibly small and she felt those damned tears swell again. What was wrong with her? Irritated, she reached up and swept them away.

"I can brush my own damn hair," she grumbled, frustrated at her apparent lack of composure.

"Good to know," he replied, humor in his tone. "It's the drop. It hits you square in the chest. It will pass," he reassured her, seeming to read her as he always did. "The bigger issue is where the hell is all of your food?"

"I eat out a lot," she replied, too embarrassed to admit she sucked at cooking.

He finished brushing her hair and they decided to order Chinese. Well, he decided. It seemed his bossiness knew no bounds. Whenever others bossed her around, it normally rose her hackles and made her fight for dominance. Everything was different with him, though. She felt as if she had known him her entire life.

They lounged on her couch and ate Chinese. *Blazing Saddles* played on her television and she found herself watching Dolor as he threw his head back and laughed. There was something so familiar about that laugh. She smiled, enjoying the normalcy of it all. For the first time in months, Kisa didn't feel so alone.

At one point she noticed Dolor's eyes locked on the picture of Adam and her that sat on the side table. An awkwardness filled their easy mood, and he looked towards her with a questioning frown.

Kisa swallowed and willed herself not to panic. She didn't talk about Adam. To anyone. Ever. "He died. Car accident. I don't want to talk about it."

He watched her a moment more, nodding at her clipped words in acceptance. She felt the tension around her heart ease a little with his understanding. She knew he had questions, but she wasn't ready. She would never be ready for that conversation.

They talked about their jobs, and Kisa wasn't sure which she was more fascinated with, his job as a surgeon or club owner. She worried he would look down at her for only being an x-ray tech, but instead she saw flickers of pride in his eyes as she talked about her life. It was strange to see that after so long. He made her feel proud of her accomplishments. Really, she should be. She was the first person in her family to graduate high school, let alone college. She worked for every scrap she had.

He opened up about a case he was debating taking. It

was supposed to be impossible, but the patient was a child and he had a soft spot for children. He was a mystery to her, and she found herself enraptured by it. They discussed his paper on the heroin epidemic, and Kisa found herself pouring out all of her views on the sensitive topic. She cried. Again. He held her. Again.

She woke later, realizing she had fallen asleep with her head on Dolor's shoulder. He had moved it as he rose from the couch.

Realizing she was awake, he leaned down and kissed the top of her head. "I have to go, kitten. Mattheus needs me at the club."

She nodded. Of course. He had a life. He couldn't just stay with her forever.

He lifted her chin, his eyes soft on her. "I'll call you tomorrow to see how you're doing. Get some rest." She thought he would kiss her for sure this time, but again, he pulled away. Grabbing his suit jacket from the bedroom, he didn't look back as he walked out of the door and took her heat with him.

Chapter Sixteen

Dolor stood, grass caressing his hide-covered knees in the light breeze. Such a lovely day for battle. He looked at the field before him, blood shimmering on the tall blades of green, much of the gore hidden among the weeds. Dolor's beard and braids were smeared with it, and he felt the blood cooling as it slid down his neck and shoulders. His thick furs held back the chill, the sunlight deceptive as the morning frost receded. His sword was pointed down, the hilt fiery in his grip. His eyes danced in excitement as he watched the opposing force gather, pulling their broken legions together for one final stand. Dolor smiled, and he knew the image he made, standing among the fallen.

His clan, although he hesitated to use such a term in his lone existence, rallied behind him. He tasted their fear and his smile grew, in part because he knew it wasn't the gathering soldiers they feared. They feared him, the legend of him anyway. A spear pierced the soft ground to his right and Dolor plucked it up, searching the remnants of the battle nearest him. With a rough stab, Dolor skewered the severed head hidden in the grass, raising it to look into the eyes of their earl. The man's eyes were a dull gray, probably quite stunning in life, and his face held the shock of a man that has realized how wrong he was about his invincibility. His warrior's braids hung stiffly, blood making them appear crimson in the sunlight. With one hand, Dolor grabbed the man's face, shoving his head further down the spear.

Dolor nodded, satisfied as he faced the enemy once

more. Reaching back and using his unnatural strength, he hurled the spear towards the encampment. It landed with a sickening thud, the spear roughly swaying as it slammed into the ground, sticking up in front of their last remaining general. Silence filled the space between them, followed by a roar of rage that echoed across the clearing. With his sword held high, the general and his army surged forward, the clanking of hooves and war cries nearly deafening.

Dolor knew the way these theatrics affected a legion and he laughed as their rage caused their fragile mental shields to come crashing down around them. Dolor lifted his hands towards the heavens, focused on the rushing horde, and brought them all to their knees instantly. Their screams turned from war pride to utmost terror as Dolor threw his power at them, unleashing all the pain he had gathered throughout the battle. Pain of their slain brothers, pain of disembowelment, pain of knowing they would never see their women again, pain of knowing they had lost, pain of severed heads and torn out throats... All of this slammed into them and there was no more thought of war, only of escape. These fearless men crawled, begged, and prayed to gods who had forgotten them, or perhaps condemned them.

Dolor's smile was beast-like as he clenched his upraised fists, his breathing ragged and his body slumped slightly. All of the energy he had poured out made him shudder as he began to pull it back into himself along with the life source of the warriors before him. He fed, as one by one, like the stars before the dawn, the screams disappeared. Bodies slumped, and Dolor stood tall once more.

He lifted his head towards God, his eyes blazing as the power of hundreds pounded through his veins. He let out his own battle cry now and felt the legion behind him flee.

Dolor gasped and sat up, his sweat coated sheets clinging to his bare chest. What the hell was that? Dolor had dreamt. Well, it was more a memory, but still. He never dreamed. He very rarely slept. He ran his hands through his damp hair, closing his eyes and taking in a shaky breath.

There were days when Dolor missed who he once was. He could still remember the feeling of that power coursing through him. The rush that came with devouring his enemies. Mostly it was the lack of humanity that he sometimes craved. Back then, the famine and death in the world couldn't touch his cold heart. He felt no pity, and certainly, no mercy.

Now he was sleeping in his bed, alone, because he didn't want to pressure a woman into something she clearly wasn't ready for. Oh, how the mighty had fallen.

Shaking his head, Dolor grabbed a water from his mini fridge. The night before with Kisa had truly rattled him. He had found himself actually enjoying the mundane evening, opening up to her in ways he had only done to Mattheus. Oh, sure, he didn't tell her about the whole immortal monster bit, but he still felt raw from the things he had said.

She made him feel. In the short amount of time he had known her, the complicated klutz had become more to him than just pain and lust. The feeling made his skin crawl, the clash of emotions chipping away at his hard found self-control. Add in the curiosity he now had about that damn picture, and Dolor was a wreck.

She was an enigma, and the vulnerability she created in him made him want to slaughter a village in rebellion.

At the same time, he wanted nothing more than to peel her open and burrow inside of her warm depths.

He knew he should back away from her. Take what little was left of his sanity and flee before she got her claws any deeper. The problem was, he couldn't. She was his beautiful broken thing and he would keep her. The monster in him refused to give her up. He had claimed her; she just didn't know it yet.

Three days. It had been three fucking days since Dolor had seen Kisa. With a heavily gloved hand, he grabbed the lava root in front of him with a bit more force than necessary, jerking it from the cave wall. Vivid violet lava shot out, nearly hitting Mattheus in the face.

"For fuck's sake, D! Watch what you're doing, man!" Mattheus roared, jumping back.

Dolor threw the plant into his bucket. They had an order for two barrels full for the pygmies, and Dolor wondered again about his choice in careers.

It all came back to feeding. When Dolor had first been cast down, he fed on the pain of mortals around him. He binged on them, reveling in the power he gained from drinking them dry. He quickly realized that doing such deep feeds, in which he fed until death took them, had unfortunate side effects. He took a piece of their essence, a part of their humanity.

He had been gaining that humanity at an alarming rate and it was unacceptable. However, stubborn creature that he was, he decided to venture further and try something non-human. Can't take on humanity from something that isn't human, right? It worked, to an extent. When Dolor had his first full feed on a supernatural creature, he realized that it was the same as it was with humans. Instead of taking in their humanity, he took other pieces from them. Sometimes it was powers, other times it was merely essence.

With their essence, Dolor found he could jump to their planes. Normally portals to Other Realms were closed to outsiders. Not to Dolor, though. The portals didn't read him as an outsider, not with that essence swirling within him. Dolor had made it his personal mission for a decade to consume a large variety of beings, essentially opening the universe to him. It was a bit of adolescent rebellion, he liked to say, although he had been far from adolescent. Things had begun to escalate, and bounties were placed on his head. Mattheus convinced the Others to call a truce with Dolor, as long as Dolor stopped feeding on them and helped Mattheus with setting up the trade.

With all realms open to him, Dolor could jump Mattheus through portals, collecting goods and making the trades. The club was neutral territory and allowed the supernatural community to congregate for goods. He thought of it as a supernatural farmers' market. Anyone that had ever had a craving for something that their usual store was out of could understand the appeal. Especially when the craving had lasted for hundreds of years. Business was good, and with the Helic region opening up, business was going to be more than good.

So why was Dolor so fucking miserable? Kisa, that's why. For three days he had called her. She ignored his calls, didn't respond to his texts, and the two times he went to her apartment she didn't answer the door. He had even gone to that disgusting cafeteria again, hoping to see those beautiful, sad eyes of hers. No such luck. He didn't know what the hell was going on, but she wouldn't sit for a week the next time he saw her.

Mattheus saw the irritation flowing off Dolor and wisely chose not to discuss it.

With the final barrel full, Dolor grabbed Mattheus' arm and jerked him through the portal, transporting them back into the storage unit at their club. It was a seamless jump now, unlike when they first had tried. It had once felt like his body was being torn limb from limb, the universe refusing to bend to him. He knew from the expression on Mattheus' face and the jagged, panting breaths that it still was a miserable experience for him.

The storage room was bespelled to the size of a football field. Joro had helped them organize it in ways that made his head spin. The portal rested in the back corner with more wards surrounding it than the pope.

They lugged the two barrels to a section labeled "Pygmy trade," dropping them beside a tall rack of strange goods. The pygmies were... odd. They mostly just wanted to get their hands on any type of drug they could find. The lava root was one of the most powerful hallucinogens in any realm. That would be a fun evening for whoever crazy fuck ordered it.

After putting the barrels away, Dolor wasted no time in leaving the room. He needed booze in his system, stat. He nipped his finger, smearing his blood along the small wooden panel that stood in place of a doorknob. The door swung open, shutting behind him and Mattheus immediately after their exit. The seams disappeared, leaving only the small square for the blood transfer.

Heading for the bar, he ignored the bartender and grabbed a bottle of his favorite whiskey. Removing the cork and taking a healthy swig, he stomped off in the direction of the thundering crowd.

Sitting down at a booth in the back of the main club, Dolor thought about his situation. Maybe Kisa simply didn't like him. That was possible. Dolor squirmed and took another deep chug. It had to have something to do with that damn picture. Who was that man? Had Kisa been married? She had no ring mark. Maybe it was a brother? He had questions with no answers, and it pissed him the hell off.

He was so used to women clinging to him, that he wasn't sure how to handle her aloofness. He thought he was going to rip through his pants during that damn bath. It had taken every ounce of his control not to take her, to make her his right then and there. He wanted her with a desperation that was driving him crazy. He knew she wanted him just as badly. He could taste it on her skin, smell it in the air.

Groaning, Dolor reached down and adjusted himself. Fuck, was he ever not hard anymore? Every time he thought about her he was instantly erect.

No one had ever affected him like this and he wondered for the hundredth time what was different about her. She was definitely human, but also not. Something dark was buried deep within her. He had seen it in her eyes. He had caught terrifying glimpses and it boggled him. Maybe she was part siren? That would certainly explain a few things.

Sometime during his brooding, Mattheus and Joro had sat in the booth with him. They chatted with each other amicably, and Dolor glared. He didn't want to see anyone flirting with anyone right now. He knew he looked like a sullen child and got up to leave. No reason to sully everyone else's good time.

As he stood, a tall human with a shaved head and jean jacket walked past their table with his friend. The man looked down at Mattheus and Joro, sneered, and leaned towards his friend. Dolor might have missed the racist bullshit spewing from him if not for his enhanced hearing. By the abrupt halt in his two companions' conversation, he knew it had not gone unnoticed by them either. His beast woke with a snarl, rushing through him until he felt his vision sharpen, the telltale sign his eyes had turned black.

Setting down his liquor bottle, Dolor followed the man to the door, ignoring Mattheus' curses and efforts to call him back.

The asshole nodded at his friend and went out a side door alone. Perfect. Dolor stalked after him, beckoning his beast's magic and using his shadows to shield him from view. As he followed out the door, he saw the guy stop in the alley and pull a pack of smokes out of his jacket. Dolor waited to remove the shadows until he stood before the man.

"Need a light?" Dolor asked smoothy.

The piece of shit jumped and yipped like a damn chihuahua, clearly startled by Dolor's abrupt appearance.

"What the fuck?"

Before he could say anything else, Dolor grabbed him by the throat, lifting him several feet off the ground and shoving him into the brick wall of the building beside them. He knew how unsettling his obsidian eyes were, and he smiled at the fear pouring off the Nazi prick. The man grabbed the wrist holding him aloft. His struggle caused his jean jacket to slide up his arms and the swastika revealed on his forearm made Dolor snarl. The man paled further. Dolor leaned forward, glamoring his teeth into sharp points as he smiled at the fucker.

Dolor felt magic swell around him and knew that Mattheus must have found them and thrown up a shield of protection. Dolor hadn't considered other human witnesses and immensely appreciated Mattheus in that moment. That would make this much easier.

The voice that crawled out of Dolor could never be mistaken as human. It was the voice that woke humans in the middle of the night. The voice of nightmares.

"Tell me, boy. Do you know what that mark on your wrist represents? Do you know the pain that symbol leaves in its wake? I could show you…" Dolor eased his magic into the man, slowly. He didn't want him to pass out on him just yet. No, he wanted to savor this.

"D…" Mattheus' voice spoke from behind him, knowing better than to touch him when he was like this.

Dolor tilted his head to the side. "What do you think, brother? Should I show him?" Dolor's eyes bore into the man's, and he saw the horror as the pain of concentration camps filled his vision. Dolor purred as he poured the pain of watching loved ones thrown into the oven, the horror of holding starving babies, the despair of knowing this was the end. The man began to scream. Dolor squeezed tighter, cutting off his airway.

"Dolor! That's enough."

Dolor was too far gone to listen. He leaned closer, the shadows of his horns projecting above his head. The man saw them and turned green.

"I have watched the world burn. I have seen the wreckage left by the ignorance of small men. I tasted your Hitler, boy. He tasted of penis envy and mommy issues. I was happy to push him to his fate." Dolor licked up the side of the man's cheek, tasting his tears. Then he said, voice barely a whisper, "and then I ate him. I wonder what you would taste like…"

Mattheus shoved him. Dolor let the man drop to the ground and fall into his own piss. Fucking coward. He looked at Dolor as if he were the devil, scuttled back, and ran. Dolor turned and punched his fist through the brick wall like it was jello.

"Finished?" Mattheus asked, leaning against the wall and watching him.

Dolor's breathing evened out and he looked back at his friend.

"Sorry." He shrugged, grinning sheepishly.

Mattheus snorted. "Did you really eat Hitler?"

It was Dolor's turn to snort. "No. But what a feast that would've been." They both laughed, and Dolor was glad to feel the tension ease.

"What's going on with you, man? I've never seen you like this. When was the last time you fed?" Mattheus said "fed" as if it should have been capitalized, and Dolor knew he meant a deep feed.

"I haven't since last year, you know that." Dolor had stopped doing deep feedings on humans due to the whole humanity issue decades ago. However, on very rare occasions, it was necessary. Last year he had been summoned to Hell, yes that Hell. One of Lucifer's generals had artifacts for trade and it was too valuable an opportunity to turn down. However, it was a week's journey through the gates, and Lucifer had a strict no eating policy in her territory. You did not go into Hell half-stocked. So, Dolor had fed.

He shuddered to think about it. Something had been off with the feeding. The man was a patient that had come into the ER. He was essentially already dead, but when Dolor had decided to take that last piece of life from him, he had fought. He had fought like hell as if he couldn't bear leaving this world. Dolor had never felt such raw will in a soul. Dolor shook his head, pushing away the memory.

"You've heard that shit before. It's never bothered you like that. What do you care what some human thinks?" Mattheus asked, pulling a deck of cards from his coat pocket. It was a nervous habit, and it irked Dolor that Mattheus felt nervous around him.

"It's the woman. I want her, Mattheus. She's... She's ignoring me." He looked up at the moon, embarrassed to have to admit something so ridiculous.

Mattheus barked out a laugh and Dolor glared.

"Now you do sound human. If you want her, fucking take her." Mattheus shrugged, turning and heading back towards the club.

He had a very simple way of looking at things.

He paused by the door to the club, not looking back as he spoke. "Thanks, D, for the," he waved a hand back towards the alley, "but no more of that shit here, okay? It's neutral territory and I would hate to have to kick your ass." He smirked over his shoulder, and Dolor laughed, shaking his head.

Dolor turned, following after him. He was going to his suite for supplies. Then he was going after his woman.

Chapter Seventeen

Dolor stormed through his door and froze. Kisa kneeled in the center of the room, facing the bed. She was naked except for a skimpy black thong. Her head was down, her hair up in a high ponytail. She didn't turn at the sound of the door crashing open. She simply kneeled there. Dolor felt as if he was dreaming as he walked around her, his eyes devouring every inch of her glowing skin. He frowned at what he saw.

She seemed to be wasting away. Her hips were pointier, her stomach slightly more concave, her cheekbones sharper. It was subtle and Dolor's supernatural sight was probably the only reason he noticed it. But he did notice. He looked down at her, worry creasing his brow at the pronounced darkness surrounding her eyes.

"Kitten?" His voice was gentle. Questioning.

Kisa said nothing and Dolor felt a pang of dread as a slow tear trailed down her cheek. What had happened? He crouched down before her, lifting her chin to look into her eyes. Her eyes. They were lifeless. Dolor felt like someone had stabbed him between the ribs. He wiped her tear away, slipping the wet finger into his mouth. Even now, he savored her pain. He hated himself a little at that moment.

Her eyes followed the movement, and a spark flared. Not dead yet. "Kisa, what's happened?"

Her gaze moved up from his mouth until she made eye contact. She looked desperate, as if she were drowning and didn't know how to swim.

"Tell me." His voice was firmer now. If she wouldn't

respond to tenderness, by God, she would respond to domination.

She closed her eyes at the sound. Her body seemed to relax, and he understood exactly what she needed. He reached out, jerking her ponytail roughly back.

"Now, kitten. Don't make me ask again."

She licked her lips, panting slightly. "M…make me forget. I need to. I need to feel." Another tear. Dolor leaned forward and licked it away. She moaned. Dolor closed his eyes, leaning his forehead against hers.

"I won't be gentle tonight, kitten. I can't be." Dolor's words held their own desperation. The liquor had already burned through his system, but he still felt unsettled. This craving for her, this need he felt was scaring the shit out of him. He wanted her to see reason. To leave before his beast could get ahold of her. He was too on edge tonight, and he feared for her. For himself.

"So don't be." Her voice was steady. Completely unafraid.

Dolor sighed. His beast purred. He stood and moved to the closet. Striding to the back, he examined his collection. Smiling, he grabbed an assortment of tools and headed back to his woman.

She was still in place, her gaze back on the floor. She was so perfect. He dropped his equipment on the bed, grabbing a wide collar. It was black with soft padding on the inside and small blue diamonds placed intricately along the front. A small metal ring dangled from the center. Dolor leaned down, lifting Kisa's chin so he could fit the collar around her neck. He hadn't used this one before, but he had seen it and fallen for it instantly. Much like he had for his kitten.

Leaning back, he swallowed at the vision before him. He grabbed the chain from the bed, hooking it to the loop on the collar and jerking her to her feet. He pulled her roughly into his body by the chain, whispering into her ear. "I want you to crawl to the middle of the bed. You are to lay on your back with your arms spread over your head. Do you understand?"

Kisa nodded, and Dolor smacked her ass hard. She yelped, obviously still tender.

"Words, Kisa," he purred.

"Y... yes, sir. I understand." Her voice was throaty, and he could smell the heat pouring off her.

"Good girl." He nipped at her shoulder, jerking her chain towards the bed. He held it just loose enough to allow her to crawl onto the bed, walking beside her. She lay on her back and spread her arms up. Her breasts lifted with the movement, and Dolor drank her in. He watched her as he stripped off his jacket, then his tie, and finally his shirt. Her eyes widened, and he realized she had never seen him shirtless before.

He ran his hand down his broad chest, over his hard abs, giving her a show. Her thighs clenched and his mouth twitched in amusement. He crawled over her body, looming above her, using his size to surround her. He ran his broad hands up her sides, barely grazing her breasts. Up her neck, over her lips, all the way up her arms and to her wrists. He gripped them roughly, pushing her into the bed before jerking his knee suddenly up between her thighs. She cried out and her back arched off the bed, her breasts pressing into his chest. He groaned at the contact, feeling her slickness dampen his slacks even through her panties.

"Maybe you aren't such a good girl after all," he purred. Then he bit the top of her breast. Hard. She cried out, jerking against his hold, the struggle pushing her more firmly against his knee. She whimpered and he released her. He stared down at the perfect set of teeth marks now darkening the creamy mound. "Mine," he growled, licking the mark.

He leaned back, reaching to the side and grabbing the cuffs from the pile. He unhooked the chain from her collar and tossed it to the floor. He cuffed her wrists to the headboard and then slid his hands back down her body, squeezing her sides firmly, his fingers digging into her thighs and then ankles. He grinned up at her before jerking her legs wide. She squirmed and struggled, trying to shut them again, and he chuckled.

"Oh, please, do struggle…"

Something in his tone must have warned her because she stopped, her ragged breaths the only movement as he cuffed her legs spread-eagled to the bed.

He stood, looking at this gorgeous thing, captive to his mercy. He licked his lips and stared into her eyes. They were no longer dead. No, now they were glowing with passion. He leaned over her, gripping the flimsy side of her panties and ripping them off with a rough tug. Her hips jerked with the movement and she blushed as he lifted the panties to his face. He inhaled, his eyes never leaving hers.

Tossing the panties aside, Dolor went back to his collection of goodies. He grabbed the next item, a wicked smile curving his lips. He crawled back up the bed, straddling her hips. Holding up the shiny, silver clamps, he savored the lust and fear that poured off her.

"Oh, you're going to like this, kitten," he murmured, leaning down and blowing across her nipples. She cried out and arched her back, pushing her breasts towards his face. Well, if she was offering…His mouth latched onto her left nipple, his tongue swirling around, tasting her. She moaned and her entire body shook. He tugged it with his teeth, and her hips jerked off the bed, her body seeking friction.

Leaning back, Dolor looked at her pink nipple, the swollen tip reaching for him.

"You remember your safe words?" Dolor growled, opening the clamp and placing it around the nipple. She nodded, and he slapped her other breast.

She cried out again, her voice loud. "Yes, sir!"

"Good." And then he tightened the clamp. She hissed and tried to move away. "Relax. It eases in a moment. Breath through it, kitten." He watched as the pain on her face softened into a lust-filled awe. He leaned over to her right nipple, tugging it between his lips the same as he had done with the left. She whimpered and squirmed, both pushing towards him and jerking away. Then he was tightening the other clamp onto the swollen peak.

"Fuck," she hissed, gazing down at the clamps.

Dolor smirked. "Fuck's not a safe word, kitten." And then he slapped her breasts. The clamps swayed with them and she moaned loudly. She was vocal tonight and Dolor delighted in the sounds. He crawled off her, grabbing his preferred flogger. He walked to the side of the bed, gazing down at her. "You're beautiful like this, kitten. Spread out for me…" He brought the flogger down against her breasts. He was gentle, knowing that the clamps would make her breasts even more sensitive. Her gaze darted between him and her chest, seeming mesmerized by the erotic dance. Dolor could relate. He accelerated his motions, the flogger coming down harder against her swollen peaks. Her breaths were frantic and her hips rose in time to his strokes.

Suddenly, Dolor altered his aim, striking her roughly against her swollen pussy. She cried out, and her entire body arched. Her eyes were wide and he reveled in the lust saturating the room. He returned to her breasts, alternating between them and her dripping sex. Her eyes were glazing over, and Dolor felt his own body aching for release. He increased his speed again, bringing the flogger down harder still. Kisa's moans echoed through the room.

Abruptly, Kisa's eyes flew wide. She gasped and cried out, "Red!"

Dolor dropped the flogger, shocked. The flogger wasn't nearly as hard as the cane. He was panting, his chest covered in sweat.

"Red!" she said frantically, as if worried he hadn't heard her.

"Okay, kitten. It's okay, we're done." He tried to soothe her with his voice as he reached up to undo her wrists.

"The clamps. Take off the clamps." Her words rushed over each other, and her eyes reminded him of a startled horse.

What had happened? He reached for the clamps, but paused.

"Take them off, Dolor!" she yelled.

Dolor winced. "Kitten, the clamps are more intense coming off than going on. The blood flow comes back, and it can be painful."

"I don't care! Just do it!" she panted.

Dolor nodded, and with quick fingers released both clamps at once, hoping to do it quickly, like ripping off a Band-Aid. Kisa sobbed as the blood rushed back to her nipples, her cries turning to screams as her back arched off the bed. The most beautiful blush crossed her chest, her cheeks pinkening as she came undone before him. Her body broke out in goosebumps as the climax took her, and Dolor could only watch as her second wall fell.

Chapter Eighteen

"Seriously, kitten? Backstreet Boys?" The look of horror on Adam's face had Kisa pausing in her perfect rendition of "Backstreet's Back." She laughed and tightened her grip on his hand.

"Don't judge me! I heard you belting out to Britney the other day."

He grinned and lifted their linked hands to his mouth, kissing her knuckles gently. "I admit nothing," he deadpanned. His eyes returned to the road, and his brow furrowed in concentration.

The roads were terrible tonight, the snow coming down in a blur of white. They were headed home from the local movie theater, and their moods were light. She was sure Adam would be quoting Deadpool for the rest of their known existence, his southern twang adding its own charm to the vulgar hero. She sighed in contentment, reaching down to the floorboard to grab what was left of their jumbo popcorn.

She leaned back, popcorn in hand, just in time to see the deer dart into their path.

Adam's arm shot out protectively in front of her as they collided, the extra strength adding support against the impact. The massive deer rolled up the hood of Adam's Honda, crashing through the windshield. The car jerked roughly to the right and Kisa felt the wheels slipping, the car beginning to flip. Another harsh jolt rocked them as they smashed into a nearby guardrail, and then an eerie silence filled the vehicle. There was a pause in time as the car plummeted off a small bridge towards the frozen lake below.

Kisa shook her head, waking suddenly. Water. There was freezing water crawling up her legs. She couldn't see. She frantically wiped the blood from her eyes, looking down as the water poured in through the shattered windows. The deer was hanging half in the windshield and half out, a mass of barely recognizable meat.

Instinctively, Kisa reached down and unbuckled her seatbelt. Her father's words about these situations rolled through her head on autopilot. "If you ever find your car in the river, pumpkin, first thing you do is unbuckle your seatbelt. Then roll down the window before you go under." His words echoed in her mind.

Reaching towards the window, Kisa realized they were shattered too. No need to roll them down. She laughed at the thought. In the back of her mind, Kisa knew she was in shock. The water was up to their waists now, the shattered windows only increasing the rate it filled the broken vehicle. She tried to clear her thoughts, looking over at Adam.

Adam.

Time slowed again as Kisa saw the extensive damage across Adam's beautiful face. The deer must have come through more on his side. Blood coated his blonde hair. It's okay, Kisa. Think. Head wounds always bleed more. That's all. The water was mid torso now. With shaking hands, Kisa reached for Adam's seatbelt. The clasp was smashed and molded into an unforgiving fist, as if the car itself had decided to commit the ultimate betrayal.

"No…no no no…" Kisa pulled on the belt desperately, trying to find the release button in the mangled mass. "Adam... Adam, you have to wake up! Adam!" Kisa touched his swollen face, trying to wake him. The water gave a heavy heave, and suddenly Kisa found herself shoulder deep in the freezing depths.

Pockets. Adam always kept a knife in his pocket. Kisa felt through the water, attempting to find Adam's front jeans pocket. Her fingers were numb from the cold, and she couldn't figure out why she couldn't find his damn pocket at first. With a sob, Kisa remembered Adam had worn dress slacks tonight. They had joked about how they never got dressed up for their dates, and Adam had beamed as they walked into the theater "all fancy like," as he had put it.

"Fuck!" Kisa's mind was shutting down. She wracked her brain for ways to push back shock. She tried to remember any other bits of wisdom her father could have passed on to her. Her mind was blank as the water reached their chins.

"Adam! Please wake up! You're the smart one, remember? I need your brain, damn it!" Frantic, Kisa gripped the belt in her frozen hands, barely noticing the sting as she pulled on it with all her might. Her eyes were impossibly wide as the car gave another lurch forward, the inside finishing its descent and fully submerging into the icy water. Kisa took one final deep breath before going under, continuing to fight with the seatbelt that was murdering her other half.

Time was a strange thing under the water. Kisa thought back to all the times she had practiced holding her breath as a child. The peace she had found in the silence of submergence. Perhaps God had molded her that way for a reason. Everything happens for a reason, right? She would find the key to getting him free. She would. Just a few more seconds. She searched the vehicle for anything sharp, black stars dancing behind her lids. She reached for his seatbelt again, blood pouring from her hands as the belt sliced into her palms with the ferocity of her tugs.

Then Kisa was being pulled away. She tried shoving the hand off her and reaching for Adam. Her Adam who still hadn't woken up. She had to save him. She struggled against the grip, but it was no use. The meaty arms wrapped around her and pulled her through the window and from the wreckage. The last thing Kisa thought before everything went dark was that drowning felt an awful lot like having her heart ripped from her chest.

Kisa stared at the ceiling, gasping for breath. Emotions slammed into her, and she tried to grab on to just one. Embarrassment, shame, ecstasy, relief, exhaustion. She closed her eyes and wished for that elusive thing called sleep. Her nightmares had been intense all week, and Kisa had only been getting an hour of sleep here or there.

Work had been a nightmare of its own. She couldn't bring herself to talk with the patients. Couldn't force her mask in place no matter how hard she had tried. Hanna had cornered her twice and tried to force her to talk. Kisa had watched her friendship fracture a little at each refusal. She couldn't talk. In order to do that she had to breathe.

It was the anniversary of the accident and here she was. What would Adam think? A sob built in her chest.

She heard a gasp and looked to the sound. Dolor stood beside her, his face so pale it seemed almost to glow, his body still as stone. She didn't dare look at his eyes, afraid of what she would see reflected back at her. She turned her face away, feeling the heat of her blush flaring. Then he was uncuffing her, pulling her shaking body on top of him.

She curled into his warm lap, feeling small and adrift. He was her anchor to sanity as he held her tightly, stroking her hair. He didn't say anything as she wept against him. Words weren't needed in that moment. Her breathing grew even and she felt a small piece of her heart begin to heal. She closed her swollen eyes and sleep finally claimed her.

Chapter Nineteen

Dolor watched Kisa sleep, her bare back rising and falling slowly. Her skin was pale, the healing welts and bruises standing out against the blackness of the sheets. She looked like a fallen star and he felt an ache grow deep within him. His fingers reached out, tracing down her delicate spine. She didn't stir. He smirked, enjoying the fact that her sheer exhaustion was caused in part by him. He also hated to admit it, but he enjoyed the fact that she could sleep so deeply with him. He knew by the shadows beneath those sunken eyes that sleep didn't come easily to her.

Dolor's head rested against the headboard as he thought about what he had witnessed inside of Kisa's memories. As her walls had fallen, he had once again been pulled into her. He had never anticipated the horror that lay beneath that gentle face. His jaw ticked in anger, and Dolor closed his eyes. He was sure those eyes were still as black as the rage that ate at him.

Dolor was livid. Livid that God could have put such an innocent soul through so much. Angry that someone else had known her touch, had felt her love. Enraged that despite the horror, his curse would not allow him to let such pain go to waste. He was shocked to realize that he didn't want to feed on her anymore. Not like that. Never like that.

A new scent hit his nose and Dolor's gaze snapped up. A form now stood just inside the door, towering and straight-backed. Dolor could read that arrogance a mile away. He slumped back onto the bed, appearing completely at ease with the sudden appearance. He sent his shadows towards Kisa, encompassing her in their dark embrace. They would shield her from any harm as well as from hearing or seeing anything she should not. His eyes locked onto the intruder, his senses casting out, tasting him. Dolor chuckled, even as more rage assaulted him. He would have the dwarf's head for this. He was supposed to have reformed the angel wards weeks ago. Clearly, he had failed to do so.

He tilted his chin up, watching as the angel stepped forward, the torchlight cascading off his golden armor. Dolor arched a brow, giving a condescending glance at the gold plated steel. "To what do I owe this honor, Paschar? It's not even Taco Tuesday..."

Paschar stepped closer, his wings tucked in tightly behind him. Armor glinted on the rounded tops of those wings and silver blades were attached to the bottoms, sharp and deadly. He was in full battle armor and Dolor's curiosity spiked. Paschar's back was straight and tense, his posture showing his discomfort. He was not a warrior, so what was this about?

"I've come for the girl."

Dolor felt his eyes widen, his brows lifting nearly to his hairline. "Did you now? I didn't realize you were looking for company. Mattheus has a wide range of nymphs that perhaps would be more to your liking. This one is a little preoccupied at the moment." Dolor's gaze leisurely strolled along Kisa's still naked body, the sheet covering her waist the only thing containing her modesty. Dolor's rage swelled, the anger roiling beneath his skin at the thought of Paschar gazing on that bruised flesh. *Mine*, the beast purred, possessive resolution flickering behind Dolor's eyes.

Paschar flinched slightly. Realizing his mistake, he took another step forward in an attempt to regain ground. He had broken rule number one. Never show weakness to another predator. It was amateur hour it would seem, as Paschar dared to reach for his sword, his fingers straying to the hilt on his back.

Anger and fear danced on his features, his words shaky as he spat, "You dare speak to me that way, Beast? If it is the Lord's will for me to take her, then that is what I will do."

Dolor didn't move from his relaxed position, but his eyes narrowed slightly, and his words rumbled as they crept across the suite. Shadows flared along Dolor's head, and a pair of massive horns began to take shape. They protruded up from his brow, two feet long and curved slightly inward. The horns were utterly black with large, sharp ridges spiraling down their length. The bases of those horns took up most of Dolor's forehead and the points were spikes begging to pierce through flesh and bone. More shadows crawled along the walls, filling his midnight eyes as he spoke.

Dolor tilted his head to the side slightly, heavy horns eating the moonlight as he murmured, "What did you just call me, boy?"

He watched as Paschar visibly swallowed, taking a step back, and dropping his hand down to his side. His shoulders trembled, and Dolor could taste the fear-drenched sweat that now coated his palms.

"I… I meant no offense, Dolor. It's just… You have no idea what is at stake. You have no idea what she is, what she is capable of."

Dolor allowed the shadows to recede slightly, his eyes remaining dark, all sense of humor now gone from his face. "Tell me."

"It is not so simple. It… it is not my place to tell." Paschar licked his lips, the nervous gesture amplified by his shifting gaze. "There was an... error. She was supposed to meet her fate, but I miscalculated. Her being in this realm is causing an imbalance. She must be taken home. If she does not go, there will be dire consequences." The fear still shone in his eyes, but Paschar looked at Dolor almost... pleadingly. He was truly afraid of him, but even more so at whatever mistake he had made and the resulting consequences he now spoke of.

Dolor could see all of this on his face, and though he knew it was a rational request, he also knew how to play this game. Desperate men took desperate action and he would not risk such things where Kisa was concerned. He would not yield and his eyes hardened further as he said, "Is that a threat?"

Paschar sighed, the fight suddenly leaving him. His gaze fell, and his jaw clenched. "You know it is not. I am not a fighter, but I am a knower of truths. Hear me when I say, this girl, this girl will bring the end of days." His eyes came back up to meet Dolor's and Dolor saw only resignation and despair there. "There is a prophecy. I cannot speak of it; however, I can assure you that she is who I seek. She must be taken back."

Dolor felt a chill slip down his spine, but he did not let it show as he gazed at his broken beauty. He traced a finger along one of her bruises and smirked at Paschar. "Well, you will simply have to tell your God that if he wishes to claim her, he can come himself. I am enjoying her at the moment."

A look of disgust formed on Paschar's face as he watched Dolor's finger, rage replacing his fear. "Even you would not be so cruel as to feed on a Sliver."

Dolor's finger paused, and his world shifted. Memories and puzzle pieces slid into place, connecting images within his mind. Kisa's hollowness, that abyss of which he had never seen its equal. The loving concern that echoed on her friends' and coworkers' faces. The brief memories he had glimpsed when he managed to put a crack in her defenses. A Sliver. A broken mate. True soulmates were so rare, practically miraculous, and even God wasn't so cruel as to separate them once they had bonded. The legend of a Sliver, of two soulmates parted after the merge, was a myth. A wicked bedtime story to keep little ones up at night.

All of these things flitted through Dolor's head in a heartbeat, and he had moments to decide how he would react. In the end, he knew that he needed knowledge and sometimes it was easier gained by feigning cognizance. He relaxed further back, a possessive hand resting on Kisa's bare ribs. A lazy grin spread across his face as he looked back at the angel before him.

"Clearly you do not fully grasp the depth of my cruelty, Paschar. Are my legends growing dull?" The angel scowled, adjusting his feet. Obviously, those legends still remained clear in his mind. Dolor felt satisfaction in that. Seeing his prey unsteady, he prodded further. "Tell me, Paschar. How did you allow something like this to happen?"

Paschar's shoulders stiffened, his pride and irritation swelling. "You dare assume the fault was mine?" he spat.

Dolor chuckled and lifted a brow. "If it weren't, you wouldn't be here to rectify the error. You are no one's cleanup crew nor are you a warrior. So, what happened?" Dolor's voice was quiet, dangerous.

"I... miscalculated. She…is abnormal. No human woman should be able to hold her breath that long. I mean, honestly, it's absurd..." The words poured from Paschar, trying to justify his mistakes.

Dolor let him speak, putting together those pieces he

had been searching. His anger began to build once more, and he forced himself to remain calm, his face exposing none of that wrath. He looked down at Kisa, in awe at her resilience. How had she been functioning all this time? Always fighting to find that peace that eluded her.

"Once I realized what had happened, I thought perhaps it was fate. Maybe she belonged here and that it was ordained. I know now that I was wrong. The longer she stays here, the more dangerous she becomes. You have no idea the power she could unleash on this world. If her shields come down...No one would be able to stop it. Not even you. Think of what the legions would do to seize such a weapon. She must be taken back." He took another step forward, and Dolor let free the growl that had been building, the ferocious sound shattering the silence, causing Paschars' face to drain of color.

Dolors' smile was sharp, the bite to his words holding more beast than man. "As I said, she is mine. You would need much more than yourself if you wish to claim her. Come back in a month or two, once I've had my fill." Lies. He would never have his fill of her. Paschar's eyes swept from Kisa to Dolor, calculating the odds of success. Dolor's grin was a predator's dare. *Try*, it begged.

Paschar knew better, and he straightened from his fighting stance.

"Soon, they will come for her. And even if they do not succeed, she is destined for destruction. It is fate."

Dolor's words were harsh in the moonlight, his eyes liquid fire. "Fuck fate."

Paschar shook his head, turning away and vanishing without another word.

Chapter Twenty

Kisa stirred, her mind slow as she stretched languidly against soft sheets. Her eyes snapped open as the memories of the night before slammed into her. She bolted upright, pulling the sheet tightly to her naked breasts. She felt wonderful. Alert for the first time in weeks. She had slept. Boy, had she slept. Her eyes darted around the room, her skin flushing as they landed on the clamps on the floor. She turned her gaze from them quickly, finding her eyes landing on something even more tempting.

Dolor lay beside her on top of the sheets. He had an arm raised over his face and seemed to be asleep. Kisa bit her lip as her gaze slid from his muscled bicep to the hard pecs rising and falling with his breaths. She had a strange urge to lean forward and lick one of his nipples. Her breaths quickened as her eyes moved lower, devouring the sight of his abs. He was hairless, and Kisa wondered if he got waxed. A surge of possessiveness swelled in her at that thought. *Mine.* The word caressed her thoughts and she remembered Dolor saying that to her the night before. Had it merely been a moment of passion? Her eyes rested on the large bulge pressing against his suit pants, and Kisa's breath left her in a rush. Fuck.

"You keep looking at my dick like that and I'm going to introduce you properly."

Kisa jerked at the husky words, her eyes snapping to Dolor's face. The gentleness of the night before was gone, replaced with a hungry lust. She swallowed, wondering what it would be like to have this man take her completely.

Dolor's eyes narrowed and before she could react he had rolled over on top of her. He pushed her back against the bed, his thick length pressing into her through the sheets. She gasped and felt her legs part for him. Dolor growled, reaching down and jerking her legs around his hips. The sheet bunched between her legs, and it and Dolor's stupid slacks were the only things between them.

Kisa was panting. Actually panting.

Dolor gripped her hands and pulled them above her head, the sheet left to fend for itself. With a wicked smirk, Dolor blew the flimsy fabric down off her breasts, his cock jerking against her as her breasts were revealed to him.

"Fuck..." His words were more growl than anything else, and a thrill coursed through Kisa. It was as if the orgasm she had finally had last night had awakened something inside of her. She felt alive. And incredibly horny.

"What the fuck is it I hear about the wards being broken last night?" Mattheus' booming voice sounded across the room as the door banged open.

Dolor cursed, grabbing the sheet and covering Kisa once more. Kisa thought she might die from embarrassment and pulled the sheet entirely over her face. What was she doing? She had almost...Oh God.

"Fuck off, Mattheus. That key is for emergencies, asshole." Dolor grumbled, remaining between Kisa's thighs.

"Emergencies like non-working wards, you mean?" Mattheus sounded pissed. What wards was he talking about? Had someone broken into the club?

"We can talk about this later. I'm a bit occupied at the moment." Dolor pushed his hips into Kisa. She let her hands out of the sheet and slapped at his shoulders. He only chuckled and did it again. Ass.

"You can fuck later. It's the fourth, and you know it's the only day the dwarf comes to town. We need to handle this. Now."

Kisa bristled at Mattheus' words. She felt a fire swirling in her veins. It had been a long time since she had felt such passion. And did he say dwarf? Before she could think better of it, Kisa sat up, nearly head butting Dolor on the way. She glared at Mattheus, whose eyes widened. He even took a small step back. She must have really looked pissed. Good. I am woman, and all that.

"No one is fucking right now, you ass. And you shouldn't call them that. They prefer the term 'little people!'" Her tone was sharp. Only when she saw Dolor's wide gaze did she realize she had dropped the sheet in her anger. She grabbed it frantically, pulling it back to her chest. Dolor and Mattheus still looked slightly horrified, and Kisa found herself rolling her eyes at them. "For fuck's sake, they're just boobs."

Dolor looked at Mattheus, who glared back at him.

"We have much to discuss, it would seem," Mattheus said to Dolor, who nodded.

They both looked back at her, and Dolor sighed. Okay, they were being super weird. Wait. Oh, no. The fourth.

"Fuck!" Kisa jumped from the bed, her feet tangling in the bed sheets. She ended up flat on her stomach, her bare, bruised ass flopping in the wind. Dolor growled, and Mattheus chuckled. She wanted to hit them both. Untangling the sheet, Kisa recovered herself and frantically searched for her clothes.

"Is she broken?" Mattheus asked, watching her with a bemused tilt to his head.

"No! I have to go. It's the fourth. Damn it, where are my pants?"

Dolor realized she was upset and told Mattheus again, in no uncertain terms, to fuck off. Once the door closed, Dolor headed over to her and helped her find her shoes.

"Kitten, what is going on?"

"It's the fourth, Dolor." She said it like he should know what that meant. She sighed in exasperation. "As in the day after the third." She shoved her legs into her pants. Dolor raised a brow in inquiry. Blowing out a hard breath, she pushed her hands into her hair. "The third is payday." Her father's payday.

The dots seemed to connect for Dolor and he nodded, heading to his closet to grab another suit. She finished getting dressed, grabbed her purse, and headed for the door.

"Kitten, I'm going with you."

Kisa turned, surprised to see Dolor dressed and heading towards her.

"You shouldn't drive today. You don't want to be driving when you drop. We can come back and grab your car later." His words irked her, as everything seemed to be doing that morning. Is this what it felt like to men when they got cockblocked? His jaw tensed as he stared down her glare. "Turn off the stare, kitten, before I put that pretty ass over my knee. This isn't a debate." He grabbed his keys, and they were off.

Once in Dolor's beautiful car, henceforth lovingly referred to as the Animal, an awkward silence beat around them. Kisa's knee bounced in agitation. She had checked her phone a dozen times and tried texting a dozen more. Her father wasn't answering. Dolor reached over, grabbing her hand and stopping her from further chewing her nails to the bone.

"Kitten, we need to talk."

She looked over at him, really not liking those words,

especially today. Her eyes must have betrayed her thoughts because Dolor flashed her a wry smile.

"You're not getting rid of me that easily." He squeezed her hand in reassurance and she felt her body relax. "Kisa..." He seemed at a loss for words, which was pretty strange for him. Dolor was always so sure of himself. He let out a breath and shifted in the seat. "Kitten, you're eyes are pretty intense when you're angry."

Huh? Kisa looked at him, dumbfounded. She knew her eyes almost turned to a dark chocolate brown when she was mad, darkening from their usual chestnut brown. Brows furrowed, Kisa asked, "And? A lot of people's eyes change when they're pissed."

Dolor tilted his head, puffing his cheeks out. It was kind of cute. "Well, yes, but…"

"Stop! That's my dad's place there. Pull over." Kisa interrupted his weird eye fixation. Energy poured through her at the sight of her dad's apartment complex. She felt as if she had drunk three cups of coffee. What was with her today? Did one orgasm really make that big of a difference? It was probably the actual sleep she had had for once. "I'll be right back." She jumped out of the Animal, heading towards her dad's building. She heard the car door shut behind her and Kisa turned. Dolor towered behind her.

"I really don't need an escort. I'm fine. I feel great, actually."

Dolor leaned forward, gripping her chin. His eyes searched hers as if he was looking for something. He smiled then, and the sight of the bright, easy grin left her a little dumbstruck. He seemed to know the effect he had on her because he ran his finger over her bottom lip. "I'm not asking permission, kitten."

Breathe. Breathing is important. Shaking her head to

clear it, she turned and headed towards the front entrance. Dolor followed, his hand landing on the small of her back. His thumbs drew small circles there and she felt it all the way to her toes. What was wrong with her? Biting her lip, Kisa reached for the buzzer, selecting her father's apartment number. Her heart began to race at the lack of response.

She had taken it upon herself to take her dad to cash his check every payday since he had been sober, taking him to pay his rent and other bills, and then grocery shopping. It had been their routine for a year. He had gotten clean, again, after the accident. He told her he knew she needed him and in return, she had been there for him to keep him on track. Until today. Kisa felt something deep in her gut begin to turn as she hit the buzzer again. Nothing.

Suddenly, someone exited the building, allowing Kisa and Dolor to grab the door before it could swing shut and lock again. As the woman passed, she smiled at Kisa. It wasn't a normal smile, though. There was something off about it. Kisa felt Dolor tense, and he stepped in front of her, shielding her from the strange lady. A strong smell drifted to her nose. What did that woman bathe in? Dolor looked down at her, his eyes panicked. What the hell? Why was he acting so weird today?

Dolor pushed into the building, his large steps eating up the ground as he headed towards the elevator. He had seen what room number she entered into the buzzer and he led her there now. Unsure of the change in pace, Kisa tried to keep up as he practically dragged her out of the elevator and down the hall. He stopped at the door and leaned his forehead against it, closing his eyes. He turned his face, pain and sadness pouring from his expression as he looked down at her.

"Kisa..." His words were soft, almost pleading.

"Move." Her voice shook as she said it.

Dolor sighed and stepped aside, his hands moving to his hair. Kisa shoved into her dad's apartment and felt the last piece of herself slipping away.

Chapter Twenty-one

Dolor had known that nothing good would be found in her father's apartment the moment he smelled the demon exiting the building. The way it had looked at them... Dolor stood in the hall, head leaning back against the wall, eyes closed as he attempted to give Kisa some semblance of privacy. He had sent his shadows in the moment they were at her father's door and knew the room was empty but for her dad. The reek of sulfur still saturated the hallway and Dolor's fists clenched. Demons didn't cross over often, especially lower class ones. That had been a level four at the most, which shouldn't have been able to enter this plane at all. What were the odds of it seeking out Kisa's father?

Paschar's words echoed in his head. "They will come for her." Was the demon looking for Kisa? If it had been, why wouldn't it have struck when it saw her? Dolor's heart clenched painfully at the sobs coming from the other side of the wall. Kisa's father wept as if his soul had been ripped from his chest. Dolor heard his apologies, his self disgust, his pleas for death as he sobbed. Dolor ground his teeth at the overwhelming pain caressing his skin like a lost lover. No. He would not feed on Kisa's father.

Deciding he had waited long enough, Dolor took a deep breath and entered the apartment. Kisa sat on the bed, numbly stroking her father's hair as he wept. His head was in her lap, tears soaking her jeans. Paraphernalia was scattered across the floor.

Kisa's face was hidden by her hair as she stared down at the man who created her.

"It's okay, Dad. It's alright."

Her words were hollow, and Dolor stiffened at the sound. He reached out with his senses, shocked at how little pain he felt. The passion that had seeped from her earlier was gone. All that was left was a broken shell of a woman. One with no more hope left.

Dolor swallowed thickly, the foreign feeling of tears stinging his eyes. It took him two attempts before soft words could make their way from his lips. "Kitten?"

Her eyes snapped up, and Dolor froze. Her shields were no more.

The black abyss was back, and back with a vengeance. Her face was nearly consumed by the darkness swirling there. It poured from her eyes in midnight shadows, seeking an outlet for all of that nothingness. Dolor took a step back. Stupid... so stupid. Hadn't he ridiculed Paschar for the same thing last night?

Kisa's head tilted to the side in an animal gesture and those shadows lunged forward, sensing his weakness. Dolor had just enough time to snap up his own shadows in a shield around himself. He shook, the energy pounding at his shield, unlike anything he had ever felt before. "Kisa! Kisa stop!" Dolor bellowed. It would never hold. It would break through and she would eat him alive.

"P...pumpkin?"

Abruptly, the onslaught stopped. Dolor sagged, his shadow barrier falling as he collapsed to his knees. Kisa stared down at her father, his hand on her cheek, staring up at her with those tear filled eyes. A broken sob ripped through the air, and Kisa buried her face into her father's neck, holding him tightly as they wept.

Dolor could only watch as they held each other, marveling at the strength of their humanity. Is this what love was? Getting to his feet, Dolor stumbled back out into the hall. He had never known love. He had never known fear. Suddenly, he was getting a crash course on both.

Chapter Twenty-two

As Dolor pulled up to the rink, Kisa noted the emptiness inside her chest. Dolor had been distant since they had left her father's apartment, and she could feel the tension in him. He was pulling away, and she didn't blame him. At the moment, she couldn't find it in herself to care. Much, anyway. The old numbness settled onto her shoulders like a favorite jacket.

She got out of the car and grabbed her gear from the backseat. Dolor's eyes had nearly bulged out of his head at her request when they had left her father's place, her dad finally sleeping off the drugs in his system. She couldn't, no, wouldn't let her life fall apart every time her father relapsed. Life goes on. One day at a time. Any cliché line she could use to keep moving forward. So she made him take her to get her derby gear out of her car and when he insisted on driving her, had him take her to practice.

She turned to head inside, refusing to meet his gaze, not out of shame or embarrassment, but out of fear of what she would see in those midnight eyes.

"Kisa?"

She glanced back, the worry in his voice making her pause. And there it was. Pity. She saw red as that pity hit her like a physical blow. He was the only one that hadn't treated her like a broken doll. She felt betrayed by that look, and the emptiness and rage inside her thrashed against her ribs, clawing at her coat of numbness.

"I don't need your fucking pity," she spat, her jaw tightening as she turned away. She heard the car door open and whirled on him, her glare not slowing him as he stormed towards her. Her chin held high, she did not yield as he neared, the fire in his eyes playing with the ice in her veins. His passion reached out and licked along her skin. Whenever she was near him, she felt consumed by him, as if he ate the very air she breathed.

Her breathing quickened as he reached for her, his grip painfully tight on her arms.

He leaned over, his breath hot on her face, "Do I seem like the type of man to pity someone? There is a difference, Kisa, between pity and just giving a shit." Her eyes never left his, the pain in her arms shooting straight to her core. She felt that core soften at his words, even as the flames within her burned higher.

"Why? Why do you even care?" Her eyes searched his face, wanting so badly to unravel the mystery of him. What was she to him? More importantly, what was he to her? His fingers softened and his thumbs soothed the ache there. He looked down at where he gripped her, his brows furrowing.

"You are not the only one to know loss." His words were barely a whisper, but she heard them nonetheless. He looked up then, but not at her eyes. No, those fiery eyes stared at her lips, and she licked them in response. She felt rather than heard the low growl that rumbled in his chest, and her heart sped as his eyes darkened. He let go of her and she nearly stumbled at the abrupt loss of contact.

She stood there as he turned away, rejection and shame churning in her gut as he walked towards his car. Her face flushed and tears stung the back of her eyes. She blinked rapidly, calming her breathing as she had done a million times before.

"I'll see you at nine, kitten," was all he said as he got into his car and drove away. She gripped the edges of her coat of numbness and pulled it more tightly around her heart.

"Shadows. Like your shadows?" Mattheus asked, for the millionth time. Dolor sighed, resting his head back on the seat of his car. He had pulled into a parking lot a few blocks from the rink to call Mattheus. Like hell was he going to leave Kisa alone right now, but he had to talk to his brother. Dolor informed him of the events that had unfolded, starting with his visit from Paschar and ending with Kisa's shadow display.

"Like mine on fucking steroids," Dolor grumbled, running his fingers through his hair. "You should have seen it, Mattheus. It was… I've never seen anything like it." Dolor didn't miss the hint of awe in his voice. He reached down and adjusted himself. Again.

"Are you saying she's stronger than you?" Mattheus' voice was quiet. The weight of the words hung in the air. Dolor was one of the strongest beings in creation.

"I'm saying she very well could be." Dolor closed his eyes.

"Fuck."

"Fuck, indeed. What do I do, brother?" Dolor was lost. What he had felt when those shadows reached for him had terrified him. Dolor was immortal and no one could match him for strength. Kisa's powers had felt like they could very well end his existence.

"Well, you said she acted as a predator, right?"

"Right…"

"So, treat her like one. Look, it doesn't matter who is the more powerful. It matters who is more dominant. You know that. Show her who's boss."

As always, Mattheus had simplified things. Could Dolor do that? Dominate Kisa when she was so lost in herself? Pull her back from that ledge? Her father had, but it had been with love, not domination. Dolor put his forehead on the steering wheel.

"Where is Kisa now?" Mattheus asked.

"At practice. She... insisted." Dolor looked up, tilting his head as a strange noise filled his ears.

Mattheus snorted on the line. "Way to show her who's boss, man. Can't believe you would leave her alone right now. She must have really spooked you."

"You have no idea..." Dolor murmured, staring hard out the windshield. A moth landed in front of his eyes, and Dolor felt his heart stutter. It was followed by another. And another. Dolor watched as hundreds of moths flew by his car and he cursed loudly.

"Gotta go. We've got fucking moths." Dolor bit out. He tossed his phone on the passenger seat, shifted his car into gear, and slammed on the gas. Dolor raced for Kisa, hoping he could outrun the light cacophony of wings.

Chapter Twenty-three

Kisa rested her hands on her knees as she panted. Closing her eyes, she tried to calm her breathing, black dots swirling in her vision. If there was one thing Kisa had learned over the past year, it was how to avoid difficult emotions. She had pushed herself hard the entire practice. She had hit every jammer that attempted to pass her and laid out any blocker that got too close. Now she had skated harder than she ever had for their last endurance drill of the night. The goal was to get twenty-seven laps in five minutes, and Kisa was sure she had beaten her personal best of twenty-nine-and-a-half laps.

Lifting her head, Kisa looked over at Sly who had been counting her laps. Sly, as well as several other teammates, were staring at her like she had sprouted a second head.

Still panting, Kisa straightened. "What?"

Sly looked back down at the clicker counter in her hand. "Holy fuck, K…" She didn't say anything else, so Kisa skated over to her, her legs shaking from the effort.

She had gotten thirty-eight laps.

"The clicker must be broken," Helliot said, looking over Sly's shoulder.

"It's not. I counted it myself," Sly responded. Her eyes were wide as they raised and met Kisa's.

"I knew it. You totally got laid!" Smack laughed, slapping Kisa on the back. "Only super cock could make that possible!"

Kisa shook her head, brows furrowing. Yeah, she had skated pretty hard tonight, but that was absurd. It wasn't even possible to get that many laps in five minutes. Even

Pawz, who was by far their fastest skater, had never capped thirty-four laps.

"Oh, Slllivvveerrr..." came a sing-songy voice behind them. The girls turned, surprised to see a young woman standing near the back exit.

Sly stepped in front of Kisa. "Hey," she called out. "We ain't recruiting. Try back during freshmeat February." Her voice was icy, and Kisa could only stare. They were always recruiting. Sly was the league's captain. She was gorgeous, with shoulder length auburn hair and an easy grin. Her eyes always sparkled with good humor and hidden secrets. She never turned away skaters. She embraced everyone with open arms.

The woman laughed. It was a cold laugh, and it made something inside Kisa recoil. Sly bristled. "Oh, you mistake my intent, little fox. I am the one recruiting." The sugary voice cackled. Her voice was almost childlike, which was at odds with her tall, slender form. She wore heavy black layers, complete with fingerless gloves. A bit goth for Kisa's taste.

Was she seriously coming to their practice to scout for skaters? The people in the derby community were some of the nicest Kisa had ever met. It was unheard of for someone to be so openly shitty as this.

"Sliver...Why don't you come out so I can get a better look at you? We are going to be such good friends, you and I," she purred, stepping closer.

Slam and Smack stepped closer to Sly, effectively making a wall in front of Kisa. What the hell? Who the fuck was Sliver?

"You think to keep her from me?" The evil that coated the woman's words shocked her.

Could words be evil? She felt herself shivering. What was going on?

"Well, there are quite a few more of us than you," Smack said cockily, putting a hand on her jaunty hip. Kisa snorted. If this lady thought to take her girls on, she had obviously never skated against the Vicious Valkyries before.

Kisa scooted to the side so that she could stand beside Smack. She didn't like the stranger's tone and she would be damned before someone came onto her turf and fucked with her girls.

"Aaah… There you are." The sickly sweet voice was back as her violet eyes locked onto Kisa.

Kisa shifted on her skates, adrenaline pumping through her system.

"Look, lady, if you want to skate against us come back with your team and we can set up a scrimmage. Otherwise, you're just wasting our rink time." Kisa tried to keep the wobble from her voice. She could feel that something was wrong with this entire situation, but she couldn't put her finger on it.

The woman tilted her head back and let out that eerie cackle again. Goosebumps rose on Kisa's arms.

"Come now. I always have my... how did you put it… team with me." Her eyes sparkled as she took another step, coming out onto the rink floor. A moth floated in front of Kisa's face, and she jerked back, swatting at it. She hated moths. Spiders? Fine. Snakes? No biggie. But moths? She shuddered.

"Necromancer…" Helliot whispered. Her eyes had latched onto the moth that was now accompanied by two more.

What?

The rink floor started to shake and the girls braced themselves as their wheeled feet attempted to throw them off balance. Sly shoved Kisa back behind her and Kisa nearly fell onto her ass as a small crater opened in the floor just to her right. Slam grabbed Kisa's arm and jerked her to her side. Her very tall, very non-human looking side.

Kisa's eyes followed the tall flow of Slam's body, now painfully lean and light green. Not now, Kisa told herself. She had had a blurry moment at her father's place, losing a bit of time and swearing she had seen shadows dancing in front of her before they had disappeared. She knew her hallucinations were brought on by stress, but this was getting ridiculous.

Slam still wore her protective gear, the knee and elbow pads looking absurdly small on her seven foot frame. Dark green hair flowed from beneath her helmet, small pink flowers sprinkled throughout the heavy mass. She turned to Kisa, and Kisa could say nothing as she stared into large, leaf green eyes. There was something strangely familiar about them...

"K? You okay?"

"W…What are you?" Kisa stuttered.

Slam's eyes widened into something akin to panic. Before she could answer, another foot-wide crater erupted in front of the weird recruiting woman. Kisa looked around frantically, stepping back towards the wall as her teammates began to shimmer. Their images shook as they all stepped forward towards the woman. Kisa didn't know where to look first. Towards the woman blowing holes into their rink or the twelve strangers who now stood before her.

Sly was no longer the captain with the laughing eyes. Instead, she was a great dane-sized fox. Her equipment clattered to the ground, her helmet falling last as she shook her massive white head. Several fluffy tails sprouted from her backside and Kisa had the insane urge to reach forward and touch one. She may have, if not for the distraction of the other creatures lined up in front of her.

Smack was looking at her, a bright, ferocious smile split across her face. "Finally." She whispered, looking victorious as she stared at Kisa. Well, at least she looked mostly human. Her curvy form had grown taller as well, but only by a foot or so. Her normally black hair had turned a stunning white gold. Her face seemed to glow, as did her nearly white blue eyes. They were the palest blue Kisa had ever seen, and vastly different from the brown ones that normally filled that pretty face.

Kisa looked away, unable to meet her gaze any longer. Helliot. Helliot still looked the same. She stepped closer to her, then faltered as Helliot held out her tattoo-covered arms. Her elaborate ink was moving. The animals scattered across her skin seemed almost to be walking down her arms. She turned her palms up and crooned at the creatures adoringly and Kisa felt her jaw drop as they leapt from her skin. They twisted and grew in midair and then there was a small army of animals before them. Two tigers, a silver hound, and a tiny blue dragon circled Helliot, glaring out at the evil woman across from them as if waiting to tear her limb from limb. A snarl ripped the air as the tiger crouched in front of Helliot. She lovingly ran a now bare hand down its striped fur.

Kisa was once again pressed as far into the wall as she could manage. Before she could get a clear assessment of the other things her teammates had turned into, a decayed hand reached up through the crater next to her. It was followed by a bony shoulder. Which was then followed by a head missing half its face. Okay. Zombies. Why not?

"K! Get behind me!" Slam called to her. Her voice still sounded the same, despite the change in her appearance. Sly's fox throat let out a terrifying chittering sound before she jumped onto the zombie that had made its way out of the hole.

"Sly!" Kisa started to move towards her, concerned about her friend. She didn't need to be. Within moments, Sly had destroyed the corpse, leaving it in thrashing pieces on the rink floor. She turned towards a different hole and descended on the next zombie in her path.

Chaos erupted. Zombies crawled from the numerous craters that had trashed their rink. Creatures attacked the zombies from all sides. Kisa looked around desperately, searching for anything she could use as a weapon. Everyone knew about zombies. Take out their head and they weren't a threat anymore. Wracking her brain for all zombie knowledge she had gathered from video games and movies, Kisa sprinted to the concession stand, nearly sliding into it as she rounded the corner.

Weapon... Weapon. Kisa searched frantically for anything she could use. She blocked out the screams and growls echoing around her, determined to find something to help protect her friends. She would sort out her sanity issues later. A mop resting against the back counter caught her eye and Kisa grabbed it. She attempted to break the floppy mop part off by snapping it over her knee and quickly realized it wasn't nearly as easy as it looked in the movies.

Suddenly, a gnarled hand appeared on the counter. Kisa watched in horror as the hand pulled the zombie's body into view. Before she knew what she was doing, Kisa had turned the mop, grabbing onto it just above the still damp mop fringes. She swung it like a baseball bat and whooped in glee as the zombie's head flew from its shoulders.

"Fuck yeah!" She laughed, gripping the makeshift weapon tightly in her hands. She had played a season of softball in high school. She hadn't expected how useful that would be.

Skating quickly, Kisa flew back out onto the rink. Pieces of zombie were everywhere. For a moment, Kisa couldn't move. She simply stared at the battle wreaking havoc on one of her favorite places in the world. One of Helliot's tigers was eating a zombie off to the right. Smack now had a gleaming sword, her battle cry sounding off like thunder as she swung the blade, swiftly decapitating a nearby zombie. Sly was making her way closer to the woman, no, necromancer, who had brought the zombies, her white tails swatting the walking dead as she passed. Slam was—

Kisa yelped as a zombie grabbed her leg from behind, whirling around and bringing the mop handle down hard onto its head. The handle sunk into the patchy blonde hair with a sickening *thwack*. With a groan of disgust, Kisa pulled the wood up from the zombie's head. Or that's what she tried to do. The zombie's neck apparently had been a bit more decayed than the rest of its body, because the head popped off, sticking to the mop when she tried to pull her weapon free. Kisa shook the stick vigorously. The head flew off and hit another zombie square in the face.

"Ha! Two points!" Smack called out to her, apparently having the time of her life. Kisa laughed and waded into the mess, swinging her mop at any zombie head she could find.

Kisa cried out in surprise as two arms latched onto her waist. She stared down at the peeling skin and lifted fingernails in horror for a moment before feeling her feet lift from the ground. She gasped, the zombie's grip squeezing the breath from her lungs.

"Don't kill her! I need her alive!" The shriek echoed across the rink, and the zombie abruptly dropped her. Kisa fell onto her knees. Before the thing could scoop her back up, she spun around and jabbed the mop stick up under the monster's chin. It broke through the top of his skull and Kisa tugged it forward, ripping off the front of his oozing face. It crumpled to the floor.

A piercing yip sounded and Kisa rose, searching the crowd. The necromancer stood holding Sly straight in the air by her smooth, snowy throat. The woman floated several feet off the ground, black and blue mist flowing around her in a fog. She smiled sweetly up at Sly.

Then she broke her neck.

Kisa wasn't sure how she heard that sound among the scream that left her lips. The snap would be forever ingrained in her memory. In her very soul. Time slowed again as Kisa watched the massive white form of her friend fall to the floor.

No. No no no…

An enraged scream erupted from the other side of the rink and she knew that Smack had seen their captain fall as well. Kisa looked at the evil being who had just murdered her beautiful friend. Their gazes locked. The woman's eyes widened.

"You're dead," Kisa whispered menacingly. Her skates felt like they floated across the rink as she moved towards the necromancer. She saw her pale and take a step back. Kisa let all the rage and despair she had felt in her entire lifetime fill her. The woman began to scream in terror. Kisa reached out, intent on ripping her limb from limb with her bare hands.

Before she could touch her, the woman imploded. She was there one minute and then gone. Her body was nothing but black and blue mist. That mist shot for Kisa, and she took a step back, frightened. There was no escaping it though. The mist hit her straight in the chest, and she threw her head back, a startled gasp the only sound she could make.

It was as if someone had tried to jump-start her heart. She had seen people who had coded at the hospital be shocked back into being. She imagined the feeling was similar. Her heart felt like it would beat through her chest and she could do nothing but stare at the wooden ceiling as pure power flowed through her body. Everything faded into the distance. She was nothing. She was everything. She was power and power was her.

"Kisa!"

That voice. She knew that voice.

"No! Don't touch her!"

How did she know that voice? Slowly, Kisa's eyes drifted from the ceiling, her head finally easing back down into a normal position. A man stood in front of her. A gorgeous man made of shadows. Kisa felt her head tilt as she inhaled his scent. *Mine.*

"Kitten? You in there?"

That word…She hated it. A snarl curled her mouth. She was no kitten. She was something so much more. Her head lowered, her chin protecting her throat from the predator across from her. She would show him who she was. And then she would make him hers.

Chapter Twenty-four

Dolor didn't breathe. He didn't so much as move as he stared down at the creature in front of him. His kitten was gone. No, this was no kitten. Kisa's derby clothes were splattered with gore, her fingers curled into claws, her eyes consumed by those obsidian shadows. They didn't pour from her eyes as they had at her father's apartment. They simply roiled behind her lids, blocking out any glimpse of her humanity. The snarl that curled her mouth should not have been as sexy to Dolor as it was. He felt himself harden further. Really not the time, he internally scolded himself.

Mattheus had said Kisa was just another predator. Looking at her now, Dolor knew she was something much more. Praying Mattheus knew what he was talking about, Dolor looked at Kisa as just another creature he needed to put into her place. He widened his stance, pushing his shoulders back to make his tall form appear even larger. He steadied his heart, which thundered with both lust and the barest hint of fear. She would smell that fear, as he had on so many other weak foes. Instead, he focused on his lust. He let it pour through him and light his eyes. He would drown her in the scent. Her eyes hooded as the smell reached her and she shook her head furiously, attempting to clear it. Dolor smirked.

That smirk seemed to trigger something in her. One minute she was kneeling about ten feet away from him, and the next she was in front of him, snarling and reaching her hands out as if to claw his face off. Physical attack he could handle. As long as she kept those shadows locked within her. Dolor didn't flinch as he lashed out with his own power, inky blackness wrapping around Kisa's wrists.

Those shadows jerked her hands down and behind her back, locking them into place. She struggled against their hold as Dolor stepped flush against her, towering over her. He leaned down and dragged his teeth along her neck, hoping to warn the predator in her into submission.

It seemed to have worked as she stilled her struggles. Until she leaned into him sensually and then attempted to bite him. Dolor reared back, a laugh lurching from him. *Mine* his beast purred, and he lifted a hand up to the snapping face of this beautiful monster in front of him. He caressed her struggling face gently before sliding his palm down to her throat. He clamped a fist around her slender neck, squeezing with just enough force to make her still. His eyes bore into hers, his own shadows coming out to play. They slid from him, making their way down her body. He caressed her with his darkness, the slithering pieces of night whispering admiring words into her ear even as his hand tightened on her throat. She wasn't struggling now. As powerful as she was, she had no control of those powers. Dolor had millennia's worth.

"Enough!" one of her teammates snapped. They were surrounding them, watching the display with a combination of horror and fascination. Dolor felt a growl rip from his lips.

"She is mine." His voice had gone guttural, his beast leaking out through the words. His eyes watched as Kisa paled and then flushed. Her face was turning the most lovely shade of red.

"Dolor!" The word was sharp, and the sound of a blade being drawn startled him back to himself.

He loosened his grip abruptly. Kisa gasped raggedly, sucking in lungfuls of air. Dolor watched the color recede, his eyes sliding across Kisa's parted lips, her heaving chest. He purred at the smell of her arousal and leaned down, his tongue slowly sliding across her lips as she remembered how to breathe.

"D... Dolor?" Her eyes were coming back, the brown creeping into the edges. It looked as if she had taken an obnoxious amount of narcotics, her pupils blown. She was returning to herself. The problem was, Dolor wasn't. He had let his beast come out to play, and he didn't know if he could push him back into his cage. Not with Kisa's power and lust calling to him. Not with her hard little body pressed so closely to him.

His tongue continued to lap at her lips gently, his hand firmly remaining on her throat.

And then Kisa returned the gesture, her tongue slipping out and grazing his lips just as gently, tasting him. His chest swelled with a satisfied rumble. Releasing her throat, Dolor gripped the back of her neck roughly. He forced her head back and slammed his mouth against hers. Their teeth clashed as their tongues fought for dominance. He devoured her, thrusting his tongue deeper, licking every inch of her warm embrace. She jumped, wrapping her legs around Dolor's waist. He clung to her ass as they consumed each other.

The sound of a clearing throat pulled them back, both of them turning with a mighty snarl at whoever dared intrude. The sight of her team standing around them in various states of dishevelment seemed to pull Kisa back farther. She shook her head again, shock lighting her features. She looked at Dolor, not seeming as afraid of his black eyes as most usually were. She ran her hands down his face, her flushed cheeks and swollen mouth doing nothing for the bulge he currently had pressed up against her.

"Mine..." Dolor growled. His beast wanted to claim her. Wanted nothing more than to shove her onto her knees and plunge into her, showing anyone who dared look exactly who she belonged to.

Her now brown eyes softened and she ran her fingers over his lips. "Yours," she murmured, burying her face into his neck. The acknowledgement seemed to tighten things in Dolor's chest and loosen them at the same time. His beast purred in satisfaction and receded. He ran a shaking hand down her trembling back.

"D. More will come. We have to get her out of here." Mattheus' voice startled Dolor.

He looked over, shocked to see his friend among the creatures surrounding them. When had he shown up? He clung harder to Kisa's ass, holding her to him. She held him more tightly in response.

"Dolor. We have to get her behind the wards." Mattheus' eyes were wary and pleading. Dolor very rarely let his beast out, and he swallowed thickly as he pushed him back even further. Kisa. Kisa needed him.

He nodded, refusing to release her as he turned and headed for the exit.

Kisa lifted her head from his shoulder, her eyes wide. "Sly..." She searched with a chocolate, tear filled gaze, and Dolor felt the girls moving in front of the broken body on the floor, hiding her from sight. Well, all of the girls but one. The blonde Valkyrie blocked the exit, gleaming sword in hand.

"Where the fuck do you think you're going with my friend?" Her words were ice and lightning. Her eyes flashed, and Dolor swore he could smell snow. He snarled, clinging tighter to Kisa. Mattheus stepped between them, seeming to be the voice of reason today.

"We have wards at the club that will protect her. This was the first of many attacks, and an easy one at that."

"Easy?" Her words were daggers. "That's my fucking friend laying over there." Her voice cracked, and Dolor felt Kisa struggle in his arms.

He set her down reluctantly and Kisa skated up to the demigod. Ignoring the glowing blade, Kisa wrapped her arms around her friend. A sob broke free from the Valkyrie's lips, and her sword clattered to the floor as she gripped Kisa harder. They held each other until the shaking tears subsided.

"I trust him, Smack." Kisa's words felt like a solid punch to Dolor's stomach. What had he done to earn such loyalty? "I have to go with them. You heard that…thing. It was after me, Smack. I can't let anyone else die for me." Her voice broke on the last, and Smack gently unclipped Kisa's helmet, tossing it to the side so she could push her hair back from her face.

"We're a family, Kisa. It's what we do." Her smile was fragile. "Be careful. You have no idea what that man is. Everyone fears him for a reason, K." Her stare landed back on Dolor.

Kisa only nodded. "Can you… Can you check on my father? If they were after me, they could go after him. Get him out of town, okay?" Dolor could hear the pain in her voice and knew she hated asking her friends for anything.

Smack nodded, seeming to collect herself. She stepped aside and shot an evil glare in Dolor's direction. "If anything happens to her, I swear…"

Dolor rolled his eyes, gripping Kisa's hand and tugging her out the door.

"W… wait! What about the rink and… Sly?" Kisa asked as Dolor pulled her towards his car.

Smack heard her and turned from the door, giving

Kisa her back. Her words were impossibly sad, and the stench of her pain danced across Dolor's senses. "We'll take her home before going to your dad's. We'll handle the rink." Then the door closed shut with a heavy thud.

Dolor put Kisa into his car, taking care to buckle her seatbelt. She stared out the window, and he watched the questions flicker across her face. Dolor sighed as he started the car and pulled out of the parking lot, following Mattheus to the club. Soon those questions would have to be asked. Dolor only hoped she could handle the answers.

Chapter Twenty-five

Kisa woke, blinking at the soft glow in the corner of her vision. She sat up, wincing as a throb began at the base of her skull. Reaching up, she massaged the ache and looked around. She must have fallen asleep in the Animal. Everything seemed foggy, and she tried to think past the throbbing creeping along her temples. Suddenly, voices breached her haze, and she recognized Dolor's low rumble. She attempted to focus on his words, but another sharp pain ricocheted off her skull. If she didn't get some Excedrin soon, she was in for one hell of a migraine.

Slowly she swung her feet off the massive bed she was on, breathing deeply as the pain swelled and then eased. Her name brought her focus once again on the voices in the hall, her eyes noting a massive wooden door in front of her. It was slightly ajar, and she could now make out a second voice with Dolor's. Mattheus.

"We can't keep her here forever, D. This is neutral territory, you know that. We need a plan." Mattheus' voice was sharp, anger lining his words.

"I realize that." Dolor's words were quiet, tense, and she imagined they had been arguing for quite some time. "The wards here are substantial enough to hide her while we figure shit out. This is only temporary, until I can decide what our next step is."

"You should have figured that out when the angel warned you in the first place. Your first step should have been to fucking tell me, Dolor!"

Kisa winced at the booming voice.

"Damnit, D, what are we doing here? We stay out of

this shit. Hell, most of the time it's us smoothing things over. You know conflict is bad for business. You jeopardize everything we have worked so hard to build. And for what? Some human plaything?"

A growl ripped through the air, and Kisa jerked, eyes going wide at the sound. Her heart hammered, and she strained to hear the words that followed.

"Speak of her like that again, and friend or no, I will rip out your throat." Dolor's voice was cool, detached, and she had no doubt he meant every word. Rip out your throat... At those words, memories came flooding back. The rink, that... woman, zombies, Sly...

A small gasp left her lips, and she reached up, covering the small sound. She was at the club. Dolor had brought her here. Dolor was...

The door opened, and Dolor looked in, his eyes taking in every inch of her as she sat on the bed. "Hey, you're awake." His voice was soft, holding none of the cold rage she had heard moments before. She glanced behind him at Mattheus, whose face still showed signs of the hurt and anger from their conversation.

He smoothed that beautiful face, a mask of lazy confidence taking its place as he followed Dolor in and shut the door behind him... He smirked at Kisa and raised a heavy brow, leaning that massive body against the doorframe.

"Not every day I have a gorgeous woman wake up in my bed with her clothes on." His voice was silk and honey, but she felt the rage simmering beneath.

She looked at Dolor and noted his clenched fists, his face peaceful. Masks, they all wore masks. She felt as if she were playing a game and she didn't know the rules. Well, she could wear a mask with the best of them.

She smiled softly and replied, "I imagine not." Dolor

stiffened, and Kisa looked at him. Was he always this transparent?

"How are you feeling?" Dolor asked, coming closer, stepping slightly in front of Mattheus. She could hear the concern there and her heart softened.

"I wouldn't say no to some Excedrin if you had it." She winced, noting the constant dull throb. Mattheus headed across the room to a door on the right as Dolor came and sat beside her. He lifted his hand to her forehead, frowning in concern

"You feel warm. The meds should help with the fever." Their eyes met, and she swallowed thickly.

"D... did all of that really happen?" Her words were quiet, and her heart stuttered as he grimly nodded. "Are you... one of them?"

"It's complicated," Dolor said uncomfortably, his hand running through his dark hair.

"So simplify it." Kisa's voice was hard, unyielding.

"He's a dog. A big one," Mattheus said with a grin, walking out of the bathroom with a bottle of Excedrin. He grabbed a bottle of water out of the mini fridge in the corner and headed to her, handing her the pills along with the water. He didn't miss a beat, as if her world hadn't just been turned upside down.

She turned wide eyes to Dolor, who was glaring at Mattheus.

"I am not a dog," Dolor growled. Okay, the growling really wasn't helping his case any. Mattheus simply snorted, leaning back against a dark chestnut dresser.

Dolor continued, "I...used to have a form similar to one. I have evolved since then. Better than a damn dolphin..." His words sounded petulant, and she could only gape at the childishness in them as her brain caught up with her ears.

Her head whipped to Mattheus, who merely smiled and plucked the ever present hat off his head. Was that a... a blowhole? A hysterical giggle escaped her, and it escalated when she saw the offended look on Mattheus' face. Wiping tears from her eyes, she steadied herself, noting the way the two men, or creatures, now looked at her as if she were insane. Sure, she was the strange one here.

Taking another calming breath, Kisa thought about what they'd just said. "What does that mean, exactly? You evolved?"

Dolor's eyes searched hers as he fought for words. She had never seen him so at a loss. That steady confidence was nowhere to be found. "Some would call me a... pain eater."

All Kisa could do was blink. "You eat pain."

"Yes, for a lack of better words. You are familiar with vampires, yes? It is somewhat similar. I take in one's essence, their energy. It has to be a particular type of energy, though, which happens to be pain."

Kisa's mind whirled. "That's why you're a sadist," she said, her voice almost a whisper. Dolor's eyes darkened then turned hungry.

"There are many reasons for my proclivities." That voice. The same one he had been using on her for weeks. The one that made her body instantly yield to him. Mattheus coughed, and she blinked.

Kisa stood, taking a step back from the bed, her palms sweaty. Was he mind fucking her? Some vampire head game? Were the desires she had been fighting against truly hers or some trick to amuse himself? "Have you... Have you been feeding on me?" His gaze never faltered as he gave her that lazy grin. A predatory glint sparked in his eyes as he noted her retreat. Predator. Animal.

"Not nearly as frequently or as much as I would like

to," he said, his voice still dark. Her jaw clenched and she straightened. She was no one's prey and she would be damned if she let him see her fear.

"What does that mean exactly?" Her words were low, dangerous, and she could see him tense slightly. Good. He should realize just how serious she was.

"I may have tried feeding from you a few times." Dolor scratched the back of his neck, grinning up at her as if to say "Whoops. My bad."

Kisa scoffed and began to pace. Adrenaline poured through her system, her fight or flight instincts making her heart race.

"Kitten... It was just a taste, really. You have an exceptionally strong mind and your walls are frustratingly impenetrable. You should know that it doesn't affect you, the way I feed. I didn't hurt you at all." At the dry look she gave him, he amended. "Apart from what you wanted, that is."

"Only a taste..." she muttered, incredulous at his audacity. "Well, I think I've heard enough for today." She turned to leave, wanting out of this room and away from Dolor before she truly lost it. She felt her sanity tiptoeing a ledge she wasn't sure she could come back from. Mattheus' large frame stood in front of the now closed door, and she felt her heart race.

She lifted her chin, staring straight into those hazel eyes. "Move it, dolphin boy." Her voice was a growl and his eyes widened in surprise. Mattheus looked behind at Dolor, still sitting on the bed. Dolor nodded, and Mattheus stepped aside, bowing exaggeratedly.

Kisa opened the door, pausing in the doorway. A small woman, maybe four feet tall, was walking past. She was delicate, and her skin had a purplish tint to it. Stunning, she didn't spare them a glance as she passed, her black leather glinting in the low torch-lit hallway, a sucker stuck between her bright red lips. Kisa watched in horror and fascination as she noticed the woman. No, not woman, for there was no way she was human. Creature.

Kisa watched the creature walk past and noted the leash she held in her hand. Almost in slow motion, Kisa's eyes followed that leash back to where it attached to a massive collar. The collar was as big around as Kisa's waist with three inch spikes sticking out from every available inch. It surrounded the neck of a seven-foot tall, heavily muscled being. He had heavy brows that nearly encompassed his forehead and his skin was a mossy green. He wore nothing but a pink thong that barely concealed his rather alarming attributes. Kisa realized she had stopped breathing as they passed, the leashed creature looking over and nodding at Mattheus, giving him a wide yellow-toothed grin. Mattheus reached in front of Kisa's frozen form and slowly shut the door. She stood there staring at the wood.

Dolor's voice was quiet as he spoke from the bed. "Your walls that hid our world from you have fallen. Unless someone is actively using a glamor, you will see their true selves. It can be… a bit jarring at first. You are safe here, Kisa. I promise."

Kisa nodded silently, shock making her shaky. She sat back on the bed, notably further away from Dolor than she had been before.

"You don't kill people when you feed?" A dangerous question, but she had to know. Maybe he was like the good vampires that only eat animals. Yeah. Right.

"Not anymore," he said, his voice flat.

Her heart hammered. "What made you stop?" It was a personal question, she knew, but she had to know what kind of trouble she was in. She had to know how bad the monster beside her was.

"Maybe I had a change of heart." His smile was cruel.

She couldn't help the snort that escaped her. Yeah, she would believe that about as quickly as she was believing the rest of this craziness.

He ran a hand through his hair. "When I feed too deeply there are side effects."

"You mean death?" She was completely lost. Was she truly having a casual conversation about him murdering people?

He smirked, and she bristled.

"That, and some that actually affect me. When I feed completely, I take a part of that creature's essence into me permanently. It can be... irksome. When it is a creature not of this world I can gain abilities. However, to feed on humans...Well, it makes me feel more human, which is not nearly as enjoyable."

"It gives him the feels." Mattheus chuckled, and Kisa jerked. She was so distracted with everything that she had nearly forgotten he was there. He sat on a horizontal, cherrywood dresser, legs crossed in front of him and arms crossed over that impressive chest. The fact that she had nearly forgotten the giant hunk was a testament to her current state of mind.

"You can leave anytime," Dolor grumbled towards him, irritation flaring.

"Oh, but this is too much fun. I'm thinking of grabbing the popcorn for the next part. You haven't even asked yet what you are, Kisa darling." His smile was cruel and she could see just how much he disliked her being there.

Dolor must have sensed it as well, because he stood quickly and was in front of Mattheus before Kisa could make sense of what was happening. Mattheus didn't even blink as he looked up at him, that wicked smile still plastered on his face.

"Well, Dolor, are you going to tell her or should I?"

Dolor was practically vibrating in his fury.

Kisa had had enough. Enough of the games. Enough of the testosterone.

"Dolor. Tell me."

He turned, his eyes guarded as he saw the resignation on her face. With a sigh, he walked back to her and sat, leaning over and placing his elbows on his knees, his head hanging low.

"Am I... Am I human?" Her words trembled, and she realized just how afraid she was of the answer.

"Yes. You are what they call a Sliver." He looked at her then and pain, honest pain, looked back at her. "When a human meets their true soul mate, it is considered a miracle. Everyone is made with a duplicate. One other soul who matches theirs completely. However, those mates are spread throughout all of time, all over the world. The odds of meeting yours, of merging those souls is…" He shook his head, looking down at his hands. She couldn't breathe as he spoke, her chest tightening to the point of pain. "When that happens, they are to be together forever. They live their human lives together and if fate wishes those lives to be cut short, they die together and spend eternity in the afterworld side by side."

He paused and swallowed. His voice was so quiet, so gentle as he spoke. "When soulmates are separated after the merge, it is considered a crime against God. It is against nature and it causes an imbalance. It has to be righted or there are consequences." His sorrowful eyes met hers. "You aren't meant to be here, kitten. You should have died in that accident. It's too late to change it now that your powers have awakened."

Couldn't breathe. She couldn't breathe. Soul mates. She had known, of course, but hearing it out loud…"What powers?" Her voice was raw, painful.

"You can end things, Kisa. Not just kill, but annihilate completely. That part of you that is missing in your soul is seeking the missing piece and it will not stop until you find it. You're a soul eater, Kisa."

"I... I... I think I'm going to be sick." Kisa tucked her head down between her legs, her breathing ragged as the world swam around her. A small garbage can was placed beneath her, and she could feel Dolor's large, soothing hand making gentle circles on her back. A ringing had begun in her ears, and she briefly wondered if she would pass out.

Soul eater. She had eaten that woman's soul. What kind of monster did that? Panic and despair swirled within her chest, disgust chipping away at her sense of control. She wrapped her arms tighter around her stomach, desperately trying to hold herself together.

"Kitten, breathe. You have to relax. Just, take a deep breath."

Dolor's movements had stilled, and Kisa looked up to see Mattheus backing towards the door, a calm expression on his face even as she could smell his fear filling the air. Wait, she could smell his fear? The room seemed dimmer, and Kisa thought she saw shadows pulsing in the corner of her vision.

What was happening? She looked towards Dolor, terrified of what she was becoming. He did not look or smell afraid. He leaned forward, placing his head against her clammy forehead and staring deep into her eyes.

"You are the same woman you were yesterday. You are still Kisa." He kissed her softly, and she gasped as his hand wrapped tightly into her ponytail, yanking her head back. "You are still mine, and we will figure this out together."

"Fuck. You really do care about her, don't you?"

She vaguely heard Mattheus speaking in the background. His words were soft, and she could hear the concern there.

In that moment, Kisa understood that it wasn't her Mattheus was so angry with. It was anything that threatened his friend.

"This changes things. You need to go see Eve," she heard Mattheus say as he moved.

The conversation was distant as the words rattled around in her head. Mates, dog, soul eater... Over and over they played until Kisa clenched her eyes tightly, shielding herself from Dolor's intense stare and willing her stomach to calm. Breathe. You can do this. Breathe.

"Find Charles. Tell him I need a favor." Dolor told Mattheus, his hand tugging on her hair more forcibly until she opened her eyes again. Only then did he release his hold, his hand sliding away from her hair to stroke her cheek. The way he was looking at her made her body flush. She should push him away. She should tell him to fuck right off with his crazy friend.

Instead, she leaned into that touch. She truly was a masochist.

His face held a mixture of concern, lust, and possessiveness. "Kitten? Are you okay?" Kisa nodded slowly, her stomach having receded from her throat, the shadows easing out of sight.

"What does all of this mean?" Kisa's voice was rough, as if the screaming hadn't just been in her head. Dolor's fingers trailed through her hair.

"It means they will be looking for you. You are one of the most powerful weapons known in existence. You are dangerous right now, but I can help you control your emotions, controlling your powers. We need to find out what your triggers are." His eyes finally slid from hers, his hands dropping. "You will also need to learn to feed."

Kisa jerked. Like hell was she eating another soul. No. Fuck that. She would control this... thing inside her. She would.

Seeming oblivious to her inner turmoil, Dolor continued, "We will teach you to control your powers. We have to figure out if there is a way to fix this. Otherwise, you will be hunted the rest of your life." Blunt honesty. Finally. She straightened and pushed her hair back, collecting herself.

"So, what do I do?" Her words were surprisingly calm, and she could have sworn pride flickered in Dolor's eyes. He straightened as well, and that cocky composure shielded him once again.

"We," he emphasized the word, "go see a friend of mine. Tell me, kitten, have you ever had your cards read?"

About the Author

Kandi Vale was born and raised in Michigan. When she isn't spending time with her husband and four beautiful children, she enjoys getting lost in a good book or laying chicks out playing roller derby. By day Kandi puts her degree from Ferris State University to use as a CT technologist, but by night she throws herself into her writing. Slivered, book one in the Slivered Souls Trilogy, is her debut novel, with books two and three in the trilogy coming soon.

Want more Kandi Vale? Join The Kandi Shop, her growing Facebook group to interact with her and her readers, email her personally at Authorkandivale@gmail, or connect with her at the below links.

facebook.com/KandiValeAuthor

twitter.com/kandi_vale

instagram.com/authorkandivale

Made in the USA
Middletown, DE
22 September 2018